Let Me Love You

Also by K.L. Gilchrist

Broken Together

Holding On

Thick Chicks

Engaged

A Christmas Kiss

SHORT FICTION

Hallway Lights

Daily Bread

Jack & Diane

The Ride

The Honeymoon Journal

Let Me Love You

Also by K.L. Gilchrist

Broken Together

Holding On

Thick Chicks

Engaged

A Christmas Kiss

SHORT FICTION

Hallway Lights

Daily Bread

Jack & Diane

The Ride

The Honeymoon Journal

Let Me Love You

A NOVELLA

K.L. GILCHRIST

For Lakeisha G.
For Tracy F.

I turned my head and saw yet another wisp of smoke on its way
to nothingness: a solitary person, completely alone—no
children, no family, no friends—yet working obsessively late
into the night, compulsively greedy for more and more, never
bothering to ask, "Why am I working like a dog, never having
any fun? And who cares?" More smoke. A bad business.

— ECCLESIASTES 4: 7-8 (THE MESSAGE)

* * *

It's better to have a partner than go it alone.
    Share the work, share the wealth.
    And if one falls down, the other helps,
    But if there's no one to help, tough!

— ECCLESIASTES 4:9-10 (THE MESSAGE)

* * *

The people who give you their food give you their heart.

— CESAR CHAVEZ

CHAPTER 1

Towanda

Towanda Mathis gazed at dancing firelight. *My life is a beautiful tornado, and I am enjoying moment of it.*

"Earth to Towanda? Are you still with us?" Shayna Stein's relaxed, southern California voice interrupted Towanda's thoughts. "Would you like some cocoa? David's buying."

Towanda glanced away from the fire pit's iron-encased orange-yellow flames. She smiled when she met her baby sister's gaze. "Caught me daydreaming?"

"What's on your mind, dear sister? A penny for your thoughts?"

A penny for her thoughts? Shayna would have to write Towanda a million-dollar check to cover the cost.

Towanda's thoughts were like brightly colored Lego pieces spilled across a table. So many. So different. So representative of a year and a half of major life changes. Overwhelming to think about, but here she stood, smiling, and grateful. CEO of a thriving marketing and branding company. Owner of a popular new restaurant. Big sister, surprisingly, to David Stein and Shayna Stein, both from the mother who had abandoned her when she was three. Gracious godmother to Benita Rodriguez, also known as Binky, a beautiful teenager bound for college soon. Best friend and spiritual sister to Binky's mom, Mariah, but only after God ushered them both through healing and forgiveness.

Towanda smiled wider and winked at her sister, but kept her thoughts private. She rubbed her hands together by the fire pit. Gazed around Franklin Square and let the natural atmosphere envelope her. Gratitude feelings filled her, but if she spoke, she might have to acknowledge other feelings tugging at her heart.

More than a year earlier, she'd hired a mega-talented, redwood tree tall, brown-skinned man as the executive chef and creative director for her restaurant, eatLARGE. Now Chef Gabriel Seay, and eatLARGE, received rave reviews from newspaper columnists, food reviewers, and individual customers via Google and Yelp.

The business growth and positive monetary outcomes invigorated Towanda like an Apple iPhone attached to a charger. But even the indescribable feeling of professional achievement couldn't compare to how amazing she felt when she stood beside Chef Gabriel.

Whenever his bass-toned voice hit her ears. When she wore the red bottoms that turned her long legs into curvy stilts and she still needed to look up to meet his chocolate kiss-colored eyes. Beyond his diamond smile. Past his caring demeanor and the jovial way he acted around her family. Inside the Hoover Dam-sized conversations they'd had about city living, gentrifying real estate, mega churches, God in America, and the urban school to jail pipeline. Those memories linked inside Towanda's mind and chained themselves to feelings so concrete she could practically reach out and touch them.

Gabriel was a man who cared and worked hard. A wonderful guy. But she couldn't make one move toward pursuing him. Because, technically, he worked for her.

Towanda stood. "Okay, I'm done zoning out. I am officially pulling my head out of the clouds. Let's get that cocoa. We've been sitting here so long my knees creak. And please don't joke about tall people and bad joints."

David grinned. "Want to give me a little of your height? I certainly wouldn't mind."

Towanda took in the sight of David and Shayna. Her brother and sister weren't twins, but they could certainly pass as such. Both with dark curly hair, though Shayna's curls bounced long about her shoulders. Compact frames and pale skin. Smallish brown eyes, soft eyelashes, and full lips. Towanda stood a half-foot taller than her siblings, but she joined them in the need to wear corrective lenses. Recently she'd thought of having LASIK to mend her sight permanently, but elective surgery wasn't something to schedule on a whim.

"You both are fine just the way you are." Towanda wrapped her Burberry cashmere cape tighter about her shoulders. Braced herself against the icy wind winding through the park. March arrived like a lion and exited like a lamb. Or so the saying went. She needed to keep a cape with her until the monthly promise delivered. "Let's get that cocoa, and I'll buy it."

David corrected her. "No, you won't. I will."

"You're in *my* city. The city of brotherly love and sisterly affection."

"And this brother of yours is going to show his sisters he loves them by buying them warm drinks."

"What if I reach in front of you and pay first?"

"I'm more agile, and I'll dart ahead."

"Are you serious?"

"Try me."

"I'm showing my love and hospitality toward you both. Let me."

"You've driven us everywhere in Philly and you haven't missed a day communicating with us since I phoned eatLARGE and first heard your voice. Sister, you don't have to spend so much on us to show your love."

Towanda laughed and linked arms with him. "Family?"

"Family."

Towanda leaned on her brother and stepped carefully, avoiding soft patches of mud in the deadened grass. Shayna flanked her other side. They moved as a trio from the wooden benches and fire pit, over to the colossal, heated, snack bar tent.

Towanda joined her sister at the slate-gray picnic table towards the back after David took their orders. Extra-large hot chocolates with marshmallows and cinnamon sprinkles.

The smell of sugar and cocoa drifted through the area and teased Towanda's nose. She loosened her wrap and got comfortable. At Christmastime, this place bustled with parents and kids who arrived to enjoy the light show, carousel, and jazzy holiday music. Months earlier, Towanda had chaperoned Binky on a date with a young man named Hezekiah. Towanda had shadowed the two without invading their space, monitoring them while they strolled, chomping on s'mores and getting to know one another. Other couples had held hands and sauntered through the area, tiny twinkling white lights as their background.

Relationships were in bloom. Love, or at least deep attraction, on technicolor display with music and lights in the background.

By February, the yuletide holiday decorations were history, but the fire pits, gourmet food trucks, and heated snack tent remained. When David and Shayna planned the Philly weekend, Towanda had typed Franklin Square right into their shared online family calendar. No lights or music, but while the trio sat and talked by the fire, Towanda had envisioned Gabriel sitting next to her, his large hands wrapped securely around hers. The imagination had been good. Better if it had been real.

Towanda glimpsed Shayna, eyes half-closed. "Shay? Falling asleep now?"

Shayna yawned and stretched. "I don't know where you find the energy to run your businesses and still see your family and friends. Sunday afternoon and I'm ready for an extended nap." She rubbed her eyes. "We should have brought Nana with us today. She's so adorable. Has she visited here with you?"

"No. Nana's into swimming and bowling on the weekends. She has a group of seniors she rolls around with. She texted me this morning before worship service and she's exhausted. She took a bus trip to Lancaster yesterday to see *Esther* the stage play. Sight & Sound. Out in Amish country."

"Central Pennsylvania?"

"That's right."

"Is it true they still drive horse-drawn buggies?"

"Um-hmm."

"And they make furniture?"

"And cheese and butter and wine and portable fireplaces and the best farm-fresh meals in America."

"What about Wisconsin?"

"What *about* Wisconsin?"

"You said the Amish make cheese. Can it compare to Wisconsin cheese?"

"Let some of those so-called cheese heads roll their Wisconsin selves into Amish country. They'd run back to the midwestern mamas crying with their feelings hurt."

Shayna's laugh bubbled up. "I keep wondering why you don't make money performing stand up."

"Because I make more money doing what I do."

"You do everything."

"Exactly."

David returned. He passed one warm, brown-paper-bag colored cup to his older sister. One to his younger. "Cheers for the most expensive cocoa I've ever bought."

Towanda sipped. Savored the heated chocolate taste. "Seven dollars per cup?"

David winced, sliding beside Shayna. "Eight."

"Only a dollar up in price since Christmas? Philly vendors must be slipping."

Shayna asked. "Do they make it from scratch?"

Towanda sipped again. "No. I'm pretty sure it's Nesquik. This snack bar is like Starbucks. When you go there, it's not about the coffee."

"It's about the experience?"

"Right." The drink's warmth spread through Towanda's core. "Who cares if you're drinking scalding water and processed cocoa powder when you're here in a circus-sized heated tent next to fire pits having an outstanding social time with friends and family? It's not about the cocoa. It's about the Instagram wish-you-were-here moment."

David and Shayna laughed and drank, and Towanda settled deeper in her chair. The irony of her own words struck a chord inside her brain and played a symphony.

Wish you were here. Wish you were here. Wish you were here.

Like a refrain from the ballad of Towanda Mathis and Gabriel Seay.

A love song that could never start.

CHAPTER 2

Gabriel

Wooden floorboards creaked beneath Gabriel's feet — the noise reminded him of an old oven door opening. Creak. Rest. Creak. He tried to lift his feet lightly as he made his way. Up to the third floor. Down the hall. Past the tiny blue bathroom. Twelve more feet to the back bedroom.

Creak. Rest. Creak.

He shut the door, took five more steps and eased his body onto the bed. Just thinking about Thursday and Friday and all day Saturday made his tired feet throb harder. Even his smile needed a rest.

"Lord, I so appreciate Sunday," Gabriel groaned, hands on his head. He wriggled his toes to slide his shoes off and they landed on the hardwood floor. Thud. Thud.

This time he kept his groan silent. Mouth open. Aunt Abigail wasn't in her room yet, was she? If she was, he'd just dropped his Vince Camuto's right on her head. If she mentioned the noise later, he would apologize. Had to. She'd been so good to him. Opened her home and let him live rent and utility bill free with only small requirements. He had to clean up after himself, fix anything that busted, and try out new entrees in her kitchen so she could enjoy them.

Her home? A six-bedroom, three floor dwelling sandwiched

between duplicates, background to the School of the Future and Fairmount Park. Or vice versa, depending how city planners viewed the street grids and property photos. Aunt Abigail and Uncle Smitty had raised five children here, and one by one they'd grown up. Launched into the world successfully. Then Uncle Smitty passed away. Man, Gabriel missed him. Lung cancer for a man who'd never smoked a day in his life. At least he'd left a legacy: a loving wife, family and friends, three sons, two daughters, and property and land he'd passed down to them.

When would Gabriel start his legacy?

"Come on, man." He spoke to the air. "Stop stretching out. You're not an old head. Thirty-five, but you're still a young man."

Gabriel rolled over with a side lean and a quick bounce. He stood to his feet and stripped down. The starched khakis, woven leather belt, and medium blue button-down shirt slid away and kissed the hardwood floor one by one. Churchgoing clothes gone. He twisted toward the window and glimpsed himself.

Black cotton socks. Black boxer briefs. Black undershirt.

Resting face frown like a clown who'd forgotten his makeup.

Who are you, Gabriel? When are you going to get your life moving at full speed?

He turned away from the window. Leaned against the bed's edge. He massaged his temples, then the rest of his face. No wrinkles or gray hairs, but the prison sentence had snatched years from his life. Midway through his thirties and he still came home to a place that wasn't home. Still slid his shoes beneath a borrowed bed. Cooked meals in battered stainless steel pots he hadn't bought.

God had provided family willing to put a roof over his head. Gabriel kneeled and thanked the Lord each morning for Aunt Abigail, his culinary school education, *and* his chance to start over.

But this was *still* settling.

He reached down and snatched up his pants. Fished his cell phone from the pocket and rested on the bed again. Called his cousin.

Michael answered. "What's up, fam?"

"Hey. Surprised you picked up."

"Surprised you called. Thought you'd be sleeping by now, with all the work you've been putting in. Where's your plaque? I need to see it. Text me a picture."

"What plaque?"

"The one that says hardest working chef in the nation."

"Stop tripping."

"No, I'm for real. That Friday video from eatLARGE is practically viral."

"That's because John had just proposed to Chablis and he danced with her while she flashed her ring. People love couples in love."

"They're buzzing over social media and your restaurant and food are featured in that video. Now every young lady from Rise Church wants her man to bring her to eatLARGE so she can order the beets with the chocolate drizzle and broiled buttered Brussels sprouts and the other fancy stuff you make."

"You're gassing me up."

"Stop the false humility."

"And it's not my restaurant. Towanda owns it."

"Isn't she a silent owner?"

"Mostly. She pops in every once in a while."

"The day to day, though?"

"All week long it's just me and the eatLARGE crew. We have Mariah with us part-time on the weekends, helping with restaurant management. I really need a full-time restaurant manager, but we get by."

"So, like I said, it's your restaurant because you're the one running it. I know you're back at work today because it's still the weekend. Shouldn't you be getting your rest?"

"I've been up. Went to early morning worship service and everything."

"My mom's still making you do that?"

"She's not making me. She used to, but I'm grown and I go and listen to the messages because I want to. And speaking of that, we're back to why I called."

"What's up?"

Gabriel glanced around the room. Wide dresser. Mirror. Bookcase. All so old they were practically frowning at him. He shifted on the sagging mattress. "I'm looking to make some moves. It's time for me to get a place of my own, and I don't mean something cheap."

"You need to borrow money?"

Gabriel scratched his mustache. "No. I've been stashing cash and earning interest, but your mom's been relying on me to stay here since I got out. She's used to me. I need to know how to break it to her."

"Aww, cousin, that's easy. Tell her you're headed back to jail."

"Not funny."

"My bad. All right, I can hear you're serious. All you need to do is let her know you'll keep checking in on her regularly. Me and Isaiah do the same thing.

"Okay cool."

"You planning on leaving the family home this month?"

"If I find a spot."

"You just said you were stashing cash. You really want to pay rent or a mortgage?"

"Yeah, man. It's time."

"Sounds like you have a woman. Do I know her? Would her last name happen to be Mathis?"

"Unless you're talking about someone else, you know I don't get down like that. I respect the woman I work for."

"With your arm around her in the video?"

"You saw that?"

"No. You just told me."

Gabriel rolled his eyes. "You're too much. I got your advice and I'm taking it. Text me or ring me if you see any affordable apartments around your way."

"I got you. I'll see ya."

"I'll see ya."

Gabriel dropped the phone to the bed. Dreamland extended him an invitation and he would accept. At least until his alarm sounded. When he woke, he would pray and shower and dress for work. Transform into charming Chef Gabriel. Put on his poker face for eatLARGE.

And keep his emotions fully in check with Towanda Mathis.

CHAPTER 3

Towanda

Nighttime arrived, and the embraces were as warm as fresh-baked croissants. Towanda leaned into them with her whole heart. She gave her brother and sister one last squeeze. "Safe travels! Call me when you reach. As soon as my schedule lets up, I promise, I will come out to Cali again."

David kissed her cheek, then stepped away from the curb. "You're staying with me this time!"

Shayna waggled a finger and dismissed her brother's sentiments. "That's what he thinks, but I know better." She gave her older sister a quick cheek kiss. "The sisterly bond cannot be broken. Dave needs understand that."

"Now, now, kids, no fights. You know better. Get to your flight." Towanda waved and backed to her Range Rover. A breath caught in her throat when she added, "Love you both."

David and Shayna mouthed their love for her in return, then they slid silently through the revolving glass door. Headed to a flight that would carry them across the sky and return them to a warmer part of the country. Back to their spouses and work lives. Orange trees and sunshine and Hollywood.

The place that held memories of the mother Towanda never knew.

Patience. She'd have to exercise patience to learn more Miriam Stein. But she would definitely learn about her, more and more, each moment she shared with her siblings.

Not tonight, though. Tonight she needed a hot meal and a quiet space to prep for Monday. In that order.

Ten minutes to eleven. In the Range Rover. Cruised out of Philly International just fine. Food? She could use the Caviar food delivery service and order spicy tuna sushi and steamed chicken dumplings. She would tip the delivery person well, especially if they arrived faster than the estimated time. But before she tapped the app to order, she'd take a hot shower and start her laptop. Mm-hm. Warm water would relax her tired feet, she would dry off and put on a plush lounging outfit. Clean, comfortable, and ready to enjoy a delicious meal alone. Caviar delivery. Yep. Caviar should do the trick.

Should.

Range Rover in the leftmost lane cruising I-95, Towanda kept her hands at three and nine on the steering wheel, but somehow she couldn't make them guide the car to the exit that would best lead her to her condo building. Instead, she zoomed down the highway toward south Philly. Home to eatLARGE.

Gabriel would be the last person in the restaurant. He always was.

He would have delectable food available for her. He always did.

She glided into a parking spot two buildings away from the restaurant. The front door was open when she walked in, but the Closed sign was on, and the dining room lights were dim. Chairs stacked together to the side. Faint smell of floor cleaning fluid. Soft white fluorescent lighting spilled out from the kitchen. She followed it like a pathway, but she didn't have to look far to find him.

Gabriel sat at a table at the very back of the dining room, nodding to music, quietly relishing a meal. Satiny song sounds of R&B played. Kindred The Family Soul. *Where would I be if I didn't know you?*

Where indeed?

Towanda took long strides toward him, her boots clicking against the floor.

He looked to her with those Hershey kiss eyes, and his gleaming smile shot a jolt of adrenaline through her.

She smiled back. Bit her lip. Gazed down. Back up. Tried to think of the right thing to say and failed.

Laying eyes on him always impressed her. She'd never seen him without a fresh haircut. Smooth. Immaculate. Just like eatLARGE itself. Towanda didn't have to poke around the dining room or kitchen. There would never be crumbs, stains, streaks, or rotting smells. He commanded his staff to work with excellence at all times, and he treated the establishment like it was his baby: with tender hands.

Did that mean he had a tender touch?

He's your employee, Towanda. Employee.

She stopped in front of him. "I just drove Dave and Shayna to the airport and once I saw them off, I realized I'm starving. Starving with a capital *S* actually, and you know I'm a little spoiled on your delicious food. I thought you might be here and have some leftovers from tonight. Love the music. I'm a huge Kindred fan."

"Might be here?" The bass in his voice sent a tremor up her spine. "We close at eleven on Sundays."

"I know that."

"And I don't leave until I inspect everything because I'm off tomorrow."

"I'm aware."

"And I might not have leftovers."

"No?"

"What if we'd sold every single portion?"

"Did we?"

He shook his head and smiled. "No."

"So. Ahem." Towanda pulled a chair from the side of the room and placed it at the table. She sat down. "Like I said, I'm starving."

Gabriel laid his fork across his plate. He stood up, laughing. "Of course. I got you."

CHAPTER 4

Gabriel

Gabriel bet Towanda was hungry. Famished. She'd directed all her energy to her family this past Friday, fussing around the front of the place. Getting her Nana settled and then finally welcoming her brother and sister into the eatery. He'd seen her take small bites of food, but it didn't amount to much. She'd been absolutely family centered. Then her friends, John and Chablis, strolled in and announced their engagement, and Towanda got caught up celebrating them. He didn't see her eat anything else that night. Peopling all weekend long and probably eating very little.

Of course, he would feed her. He couldn't make his hands move fast enough to retrieve cutlery and a white cloth napkin for her while her meal warmed. Roasted chicken with herbed purple smashed potatoes. Broccolini with green beans, green apples, and avocado. Ice-cold Perrier poured fresh for her to drink.

Gabriel set it all before Towanda with a flourish. "Eat. Please."

"I know you're not done." She waved her fork in the air. "Sit and finish your food."

"Huh?"

Her face lit with a smile. "You're still standing there. Come on. Have a seat."

He sat down. "Oh, yeah."

Gabriel tried to stop staring. Her hair looked fantastic tonight, though. Caramel-tinted and wild, curling about her head like a lion's mane.

This woman. Mm-hmm. This grown woman.

This grown woman probably had no idea how powerfully she'd clicked into the room. Husky voice. Darn near lethal curves on her tall body. Snatched his attention in nanoseconds.

They ate together quietly. He chewed roasted chicken and stole glimpses at her.

She nibbled the broccolini first, then devoured the purple potatoes, scooping them up fast and leaving growing white space in her plate. Obviously her favorite. He would remember. Most definitely, he'd remember.

"The building next door is up for sale now. Prime real estate." Towanda picked up her water and sipped.

"Uh-huh. I hear that brain grinding."

"I'm an entrepreneur."

"The best."

"I keep an eye out for excellent investments."

"Surely."

"What do you think?"

"Me?"

"We're the only two here."

"Costs too much."

"Really?"

"Just my opinion."

Towanda finished her potatoes, took three more nibbles of the broccolini, then rested her fork atop the chicken. "Tell me why you think it costs too much. Share your reasoning."

Gabriel chewed and swallowed. The chicken seemed dry. Maybe she wouldn't notice. Mushroom sauce was terrific though. "It's only a townhouse, but it's on the market for 989K, with almost 11 thou per year taxes. Let's assume you get a thirty-year mortgage and rent it out as a brand new landlord, you'd have to find someone willing to pay almost

$4300 per month on a fixed mortgage just because some genius filled the place with oak hardwood flooring and a finished rooftop with an outdoor shower so someone can exercise up there and then shower outside before they come downstairs to their four-bedroom home with a two HVAC system and all that would be well and good except I know the type of people that place is catering to and it won't be anyone of color trying to stay in the same Philadelphia neighborhood they were raised in. The price doesn't need to be darn near a million dollars for a building on a grimy city street that hasn't gotten any bigger in a century."

"Wow."

"You asked."

"I did."

"How's the chicken?"

Towanda speared a forkful and chewed. "The mushroom flavor is amazing, but the texture is a little dry."

"My apologies."

"No worries. The chef is a friend of mine. He'll do better next time."

"Thanks."

"Still against me adding to my real estate portfolio if it involves any type of gentrified spots?"

Gabriel shrugged. "Listen, this is Philly. Your money. Your investments. But if I were to invest in real estate—"

"It wouldn't be an overpriced city townhouse."

"Nope."

"Seems like that's all we're seeing down here."

He shrugged again. "Restaurants. Pet spas. Smoke shops."

"Ice cream parlors."

"Diners."

"Competition?"

"Dead wrong."

"Come again?"

She lay her fork down, covered her mouth, and yawned. Slow as a well-fed Siamese cat. "No diner can compete with your food.

eatLARGE has the best chef in this town. You can battle anybody. I don't care who you tell."

"Isn't that from a hip-hop song?"

"LL. Old school. Lord knows I don't listen to any ratchet music designed to make strippers shake."

The background music changed. Kindred faded out and passed the mic to Anthony Hamilton crooning "Charlene".

He asked. "But you like this one, though? More your speed?"

She rocked her shoulders. Moved with the groove. "Definitely. Is this your Spotify playlist?"

"Guilty."

"You have great taste in tunes."

"Wish music would adopt me."

"That's from Erick Sermon."

"I was testing you, since you seem to know quite a few lyrics."

His eyes brushed over her form. Seated. Smart. Statuesque. Soft wrap dress with matching boots. Loving her meal. Valuing his opinions. Grooving to music. Making him feel like he was too close to an open flame inside a moment that included a soundtrack.

Gabriel stood and snatched his phone. He silenced it before sliding it into his pocket. He got busy once again, collecting his plate and cutlery.

The corners of her mouth turned down and her brow furrowed.

He glimpsed the annoyed look and explained. "I gotta finish up in here. It's getting late."

Towanda passed her empty plate. "What would you invest in?"

"Not city townhouses."

"What then?"

Dishes in the kitchen's stainless steel sink, he grabbed the water hose, thankful she'd let him design an island-style layout for the kitchen. This way, the cleaning area moved him yards away from the dining room.

"Hello!" her voice reached into the kitchen and tapped his ear.

"Investing?" he called back.

"Yes."

Gabriel cleaned the dishes fast and grabbed a barkeepers towel to wipe his hands and forearms. Kitchen clean. Dishes done. With the restaurant sanitized by the eatLARGE staff and inspected by him before Towanda arrived, he could exit in peace. He had to leave. Now. The visual of Towanda rocking to music — it stirred up too many feelings. Had him entertaining thoughts more aromatic than a kettle full of spicy jambalaya.

Could he ask her to follow him home? No way. That wouldn't be right for more reasons than one. This was a woman who lived in a gorgeous Center City condo. Not that he'd ever visited, but he'd heard about it. The idea of inviting her to his aunt's well-kept but aging West Philly row home made him cringe.

Understanding that he and Towanda must maintain a professional relationship extinguished the thought completely, like salt poured onto a grease fire.

"I'm a busy man," Gabriel said.

"And that means?"

"I'd do what busy investors do." He called out and dashed to his tiny office to get his jacket and bag. "I would invest in assets that will only appreciate. Land. Gold. Cobalt."

"Why cobalt?"

He grinned. "You ain't know about cobalt?"

She stood up. "Enlighten me."

He led the way out, quickly shutting off the lights and guiding her through the darkened front room. Halfway to the door, she stood closer to him. He relaxed his hand on instinct. She didn't reach for it, and he swallowed a mixture of relief and disappointment.

He said, "Cobalt is inside every lithium-ion battery. Every electric vehicle. I'm planning to invest in cobalt and send Elon Musk a thank-you card every fiscal year."

"Hamilton never told me cobalt would be a brilliant investment."

Hamilton?

Gabriel ushered Towanda to the front step. The key almost slipped from his hand when he locked the door.

He asked what his mind demanded, "Who's Hamilton?"

"Hamilton Munroe. My financial advisor — been advising me for years. Come on, you've heard me talk about him. He visited a few months back, and you shook hands with him. He had dinner with me and asked for two to-go orders of Brussels sprouts and apple hash."

Gabriel exhaled. Boss or not, he would definitely stomp out his growing feelings if she had a man. "Oh yeah. Old dude with the fedora. I remember him now."

"Old dude? He's not that old. Fifty is the new forty."

"And thirty-five is the new... twenty-five?"

"I hope so, because I'm not getting any younger."

"True."

On the sidewalk facing her, he ran out of words, so he stared. Unapologetically. Burberry wrap. Makeup done so smooth and perfect it only enhanced her face. Not cute. Not beautiful. Striking. Graceful. Plus she was astoundingly smart and degreed and liked to stop through and chat with him.

Man, stop. Go home. Now.

Gabriel pointed. "Yeah, um, my truck is down the way."

"I'm over here. I don't know how I was blessed enough to find a spot so close to the restaurant."

"Yeah."

"Thanks for the delicious dinner."

"You know you can stop in anytime for a meal. I got you."

She gazed in his eyes. "You do."

Why couldn't they exist in a different space and time? If he weren't still building his life. If he owned condos, investments, and multiple businesses. If he didn't serve as the executive chef slash creative director slash manager of her restaurant.

If all that weren't true.

Well...

He would escort her to jeweler's row in the morning, let her pick out any diamond she wanted, whisk her away on a flight to Aruba, get married overlooking blue-green water, relish the honeymoon, and then fly back to Philly to ask her Nana what color she'd like them to paint her very own wing of their renovated Wyncote mansion.

Gabriel snapped out of that fantasy and was left looking at a frowning Towanda. Late model Range Rover gleaming in the background.

He mumbled. "Goodnight."

She turned away. "'Night."

Chilled air caressed his face. He trudged down the street to his beat-up Expedition and settled his mind with bottom line thoughts.

Towanda needed a high value man.

It sure wasn't him.

CHAPTER 5

Towanda

If Towanda believed in past lives, which she didn't because the idea was ridiculous, she'd think she was once married a rich-skinned king named Gabriel. A man who stood head and shoulders above the crowd. They must have ruled their land together benevolently.

Fast forward to last night and the king and queen ate a dinner fit for royals complete with musical accompaniment.

So Gabriel loved neo-soul? His Spotify playlist probably included Jill Scott's "A Long Walk". Why did he end their mealtime so soon? If Towanda had stayed longer, maybe they could have split dessert. eatLARGE served a wicked-tasting vegan chocolate cake with creamy chocolate ganache icing. Towanda had eaten none with Gabriel, but she would certainly enjoy indulging.

"I have to stop thinking about anything like that." She sighed and scanned her laptop screen. "I cannot fall in love. I don't care if that man serves me ambrosia from heaven. LARGE Enterprises signs his paychecks. God will provide me with a love of my own, but Gabriel Seay can't be it. I'll continue loving his food and that's it."

"Are you in here talking to yourself again? I've told you about that."

Who else but Jackie would knock only once and completely push Towanda out of her thoughts?

Towanda waved in her office manager. "I'm processing some things. I'm not crazy."

"Glad to hear that, but I can't call you crazy anyhow."

"No?"

"It's not politically correct to use an outdated stereotypical term to make fun of potential mental health issues. I'm here to ask if you've been answering your business cell number?"

"Monday through Saturday, of course."

"And your personal phone?"

"Always, except I didn't look at it last night and I've been trying to keep my early morning technology-free in favor of reading my Bible in peace."

Jackie made a face and sighed. "Then I think I know why the think-LARGE main voice mail is filled with messages from Mariah."

"Oh, Lord." Towanda reached over and snatched her purse from the edge of her desk. "She must have been trying to reach me all last night, and I was in la-la land somewhere over the rainbow and—"

"And?" Jackie drawled and raised her thick eyebrows. "Go on. Something about rainbows?"

Towanda tapped her phone screen. Mariah was the second entry in her favorite list, right beneath Nana's number. "Forget about the rainbows. I'm calling the bestie back now."

"But the rainbows, though?"

"Jackie!"

"You need to be in the conference room in fifteen minutes and tell Mariah I said hello."

Towanda nodded and watched her office door click shut while she waited for her best friend to answer. Jackie. She behaved more like a godmother than an office manager. Towanda still didn't want to disclose those pesky attraction feelings for Gabriel. Jackie probably sensed it, though. Woman's intuition.

Mariah answered the call, out of breath. "T!"

"Hey, Jackie said you left messages on the main voice mail?"

"Yeah."

"Why?"

"We're having lunch today. Did you forget?"

"Uh... that's this week?"

"You forgot. I knew it. You didn't call me back after you dropped off your family at the airport. No return texts. Had me thinking something happened to you?"

Towanda closed her eyes. eatLARGE. Gabriel's handsome face. The delectable taste of his food. Kindred's soulful voices in song.

Where would I be if I didn't know you?

Mariah prompted. "T?"

"I'm here." Towanda yanked her thoughts from last night to the present day. "Sorry I worried you. I stopped past eatLARGE at closing time and then I was exhausted when I reached home."

"eatLARGE?"

"Yes."

"After hours?"

"Yes, but listen, I had a reason to go, and—"

"Uh-huh. Say no more. I'll see your face at the Saladworks at one o'clock."

"I'll be there."

Towanda ended the call and placed her phone on the desk. Mariah. Yet another person who could see right through her and sense something was different.

She would have no problem bringing it up.

"Talk to me." Mariah cut into a bountiful bowl of garden goodness with her knife and fork, shredding her meal into smaller bites. "Spill it all out now in the safety of my presence."

Towanda pushed her own fork through two tiny grilled shrimp. "Nothing to spill."

"There has to be."

"What makes you think that?"

"You're so attached to your phone I'm surprised you're not invested in a company designed to wire SIM cards into earlobes. You never miss calls. Why do you think I freaked out last night and started calling everywhere?"

"Because you have me mixed up with your teenage daughter, super mommy."

Mariah munched salad, chewed and swallowed. "Confession is good for the soul."

"Before we take a swan dive into my world, tell me how you're doing?" Towanda lowered her voice. "How are you and Oscar? And what's going on with your AA meetings?"

Mariah's eyes shifted this way and that. Like she had plenty to say, but not enough time to say it. "Oscar and I are much better than we were last year. We're taking life one day at a time, but we'll go to Council for Relationships long before we file for a divorce. I can say that. And I'm still getting out to AA twice a month."

"Wonderful!"

Mariah pointed her fork at Towanda. "Now you! Talk."

Towanda glanced around. Not one person in the vicinity that she recognized from eatLARGE or Rise Community Church or any of her networking associations. She leaned in. "Gabriel's food is seducing me."

"Wha-a-t?"

"Last night was the third time I let myself drive to eatLARGE when I knew he'd be alone. Girl, he made my plate and fed me so well, like he always does."

"You're using dinner as an excuse to stalk him?"

"Can you not use the *S* word?"

"You're stalking him."

"I like his food."

"I like his food. Philly likes his food. *You* like more than his food."

"It's not just the food. When I pass through, he treats me like a queen. He listens to Kindred and Anthony Hamilton and I'm guessing he likes Jill Scott too, but anyway, he always walks me to my ride and he thinks about everything so critically and there's tenderness in his movements." Towanda paused. Mixed green goddess dressing into her lettuce leaves. Stopped. Mixed again. "He works for me."

"I'm so happy you understand that."

"He works for me." Towanda sighed and scooped shredded carrot onto her fork.

"Don't be so hard on yourself. Say he didn't work for you? What then?"

Towanda grinned. "I'd let it be known that I wouldn't mind going out with him. We have chemistry. Our backgrounds are different, but I think it could work as long as we respect one another."

"You don't care at all that he went to prison?"

"He was a teenager who got caught up in the drug game, but he finished his jail time and he's a man now. I've never seen him so much as smoke a cigarette. Being a chef is his life. You work around him. You see how much effort he puts into eatLARGE. He's fully responsible for the restaurant's success."

"Do you think he might know how much of a gap there is between what you make and what he makes?"

"Maybe."

"All I'm saying is, that type of thing can mess with men."

Towanda split open her wheat roll and tossed Mariah's words from side to side in her brain. All men weren't that prideful. Gabriel had never treated Towanda like a boss, anyway. From the moment contractors hammered the last nail into the eatLARGE's interior, to when the two of them dashed around the restaurant putting flowers on the community table and plants on the windowsills, they'd behaved as equals. She had money. So what? Their gentleness with one another and their work ethics matched.

Towanda spread butter on her roll. "The difference between my net worth and his net worth isn't the issue. The issue is I'm not in the market for falling in love with a co-worker, and neither Gabriel nor I need the complications that come with dating. eatLARGE is more than a restaurant to him, that much I know, and as long as he's there, I'm only his employer."

Pilates class at City Fitness. Towanda's words from her conversation with Mariah remixed themselves in her brain while she pushed herself during repetitions of forearm plank to dolphin.

Class ended, and she stood, glowing body, relaxed from her scalp to her toes. She walked to the locker room, smiling. Content.

Yes, she could co-exist with her thoughts and still maintain control.

Yes, she could be attracted to Gabriel and not make a move toward dating him.

"Deep breath in." Towanda inhaled to a count of seven. "Out..." She exhaled and used her hand towel to mop sweat trickling down her forehead. She plunked down on the locker room bench and pulled her phone from her gym bag. Scrolled through her messages.

She laughed. "Mariah was right. I am a slave to my phone... and what is this? Will we see you at Red, White, and Blue?"

She adjusted her glasses and tapped the email message.

"Lilianne," Towanda muttered. "I should have known. Who else would send a family reunion message that looks like an invitation to the White House?"

Towanda's fingers gripped her phone. Her brain picked out the details. Greetings and blessings. Cordially invited. Bring a guest. First annual Red, White, and Blue Excellence Extravaganza. Weaving together the pieces of our family history. Martha's Vineyard. Fourth of July weekend.

Lilianne. Auntie Reecie and Uncle Charles' daughter. Cousin Lilianne and her well-to-do brood were inviting family and guests to Martha's Vineyard for an Independence Day themed family reunion.

Towanda whistled and slid her phone into her Nike bag. "Lilianne? An email invitation? Bougie does email invitations now? Tsk. Tsk. Tsk." She pulled her on her gray sweatshirt and shoved her feet into Nike slides. "She must be losing her touch."

At her condo, Towanda snatched the engraved linen invitation from her mailbox and smirked.

"So I was wrong. I can accept that. And Lord knows I need a spouse because I've got to stop this talking to myself."

In her kitchen, Towanda blended a banana and strawberry protein smoothie. She stood at the counter, drinking it and reading the invitation at the same time. The formal invitation contained more than the email. It detailed the entire event. Red, White, and Blue Excellence meant Lilianne and her family were presenting a combination summer picnic, fashion gala, and gospel brunch.

Towanda and Lilianne hadn't gotten along since they were kids, and for years Lilianne had remained uncommunicative with her. Was it Towanda's fault she was Nana's favorite grand baby? No. Was it Towanda's fault she'd followed in Nana's footsteps and became the family's next female entrepreneur? No. But Lilianne wouldn't hold a large scale family event without her grandmother present and accounted for, and Nana would never go without Towanda.

Towanda had to attend whether or not she wanted to. She would call Nana first, then RSVP.

She flipped to the second page of the invitation. She scanned the hand-written note attached to the information page and her temperature shot up.

> *Hello, Cousin Towanda! Please don't stress over a date for the event, as I know you're incurably single. You can R.S.V.P. for yourself with Nana as your plus one. I've already made my assistant aware of the room block arrangements. We're looking forward to seeing you both in July.*
> *Best regards,*
> *Mrs. Lilianne Waters-Winters*

Towanda crushed the note in her palm. She dropped it and the invitation to the counter and left them there. If Yolanda, the cleaning lady, found it and discarded it tomorrow, oh well.

Towanda paced the kitchen. The living room. The hallway. Her office.

Incurably single, huh? Oh, no she didn't!

Single. Yes.

Incurable. No.

She didn't have a significant situation at the moment, but there was certainly someone who could look her in the eyes and give her the feels. She'd felt the flow of respect and friendship and attraction, and Lilianne needed to see that.

Even if she only saw it for one weekend.

CHAPTER 6
Gabriel

"No! Absolutely not! I'm not the right person. Ask someone else."

Gabriel's words hit the air loud and clear to his ears and, hopefully, to hers. Why did she look so stunned? He hadn't yelled. Why did she shuffle back like he'd pushed her? Maybe he'd been too curt. He'd only been that direct because she was a no-nonsense person. All business. She understood a plain, crystal-clear answer. Even if he had delivered it while nursing a cloudy heart.

Now she was steaming. Perfect. If he stayed in the dining room, he'd have to endure her hate vibes. He'd retreat. Let her sort it out. She might act like she'd been sucking on lemons, but she'd get over it. Let her take a few deep breaths and get out of her feelings. Their friendship and his career would remain intact.

Gabriel swooped up his laptop, snatched his handful of yellow sticky notes from the table, and stalked over to his office. The place he mostly used for talking to his staff privately and storing his personal items because the square footage was meant for a person half his size. He plopped into his office chair and re-organized his sticky notes, placing them in neat rows across the desk. The cooks, servers, and other staff wouldn't arrive for a while. He'd have peace for at least another hour.

Back to the new entrée plans. Recent restaurant feedback centered on requests for additional vegan dishes. The restaurant wasn't 100% vegan, but 50% of the menu items were vegan-friendly. That used to be enough to please the vegan community. Not any more. According to the YELP comments, vegans definitely wanted more variety. With maximum flavor and a touch of decadence. The eatLARGE touch by Chef Gabriel and company.

Towanda arrived and loomed in the doorway. Those long legs placed her in front of his desk too fast for him to flee.

He slid his reading glasses down his nose and looked up. "May I help you?"

She glared. "I can't believe you ran away from me!"

"You asked me to be a fake plus one for your cousin's glam party weekend. I'm a restaurant professional, not an escort."

"It's not a glam party. It's a family reunion."

"With a fashion gala?"

"My family does it big."

"And a white party? And a gospel brunch?"

"Yes."

"Just so I'm completely clear, I'd have to wear an all white linen outfit on Saturday and a blue suit when the gospel choir sings on Sunday. Let me guess. Friday I'd have to wear red?"

"Lilianne likes everyone to dress the same. It'll look better in the photo books. All the attendees will receive a copy."

He sighed. "Let me play devil's advocate. If I attended, I would attend as who or what?"

She took two steps forward. "As my friend and special guest, and I should add, Philly's favorite chef."

"I wouldn't go that far."

"Do we read the same *Philadelphia Tribune* articles?"

"It would be a date of convenience."

She bit her lip. Scanned his face. "You know, you're really making me feel great. I'll be honest with you. Lilianne is *that* cousin. The one who can't wait to see me walk in solo, and I... don't want to give her the satisfaction. You're my friend and... I kind of need you."

"Attend as your friend?"

She nodded. "And Nana's friend because she'll be there too and she'd love you to come. Please."

He drummed his fingers on the desktop. Why did she bring up Nana? Man, did he love her. Spunky spirit, fly clothes, and all. Whenever she came around, as far as he was concerned, she was his grandmother, too.

Gabriel studied the wall behind Towanda. It was the color of storm clouds and way too empty. Pictures could liven it up. Pics of family. Of babies. Kids. Photos snapped on excursions with friends. Something. Anything that showed his life was more than unique food creations, training new cooks, and restaurant work.

He tugged his mustache and looked at Towanda's face. Still striking. Still dead serious. She'd pulled her hair into a bun so tight it narrowed her eyes. Cherry-stained lips, crisp white button-down shirt, and pants the shade of black licorice. Giving him that fashion week appearance.

A grown woman who definitely needed a high-value man.

God help me.

He pushed his laptop aside and slumped in his chair. "Nana?"

Towanda nodded. "Nana."

Dang, she was making it hard for a brother to say no. But what if he traveled there for the weekend and couldn't control himself? What if he mixed in with her family and the sun went down and his heart fell into an arena called *boyfriend*? Would party and dance time pull them into a feeling called *engaged*? Or at midnight with the shades drawn? Would he feel married?

He had held and rocked her when her brother phoned last year. He'd absorbed her vulnerability and remained cool. Rested his arms around her body again when David and Shayna visited — another critical time. He'd still behaved like a gentleman.

If they didn't fall into anything inappropriate these last few months, three days on Martha's Vineyard with Nana and her relatives probably wouldn't change anything.

Family dinner. A gala and a brunch with gospel greats. Nana between them.

Gabriel stopped himself from making prayer hands and sat up straight. "Okay."

"Okay?"

"I'll be there for you."

She smiled. "We're in this together?"

"You can count on me."

CHAPTER 7

Towanda

Towanda shifted her gaze to the front of the exercise room. Eyes front because all she wanted to do was perform Pilates with intentional movement. Let her body do its best.

She could ignore Mariah's sweat-glistened expression if she could keep her head turned ever so slightly to the right long enough.

The expression that shouted, *you know better.*

Glute bridge with arm reach and heel raise.

Mariah loud-whispered. "Tell him you changed your mind. I mean, you don't have to lie to him or act like you have another date or anything like that. Say that you've had some time to think and you're reneging for professional reasons. But you should probably tell him today before any more time passes."

Towanda tried to keep her hips steady. Her breath even.

Mariah cranked up the loud-whisper. "I know I sound like a hater and, don't get me wrong, we all like Gabriel, but your hormones are messing with your common sense and you're not even considering the ramifications."

"Ramifications?" Towanda dropped her hips to the mat and stared Mariah. "What ramifications?

"Ladies." Pilates teacher Susanne crept toward them, shaking her head and pursing her lips. Giving the international *shh* signal. "Voices, ladies."

Towanda flashed Mariah a *quiet* expression and nodded at Susanne. They'd keep their voices low. Certainly. That's how Towanda wanted it, anyway.

Roll back with alternating elbow reach back.

Mariah kept her lips closed for the rest of the class. She inhaled and exhaled with each pose, but didn't loud-whisper another comment to Towanda.

Afterward, Towanda rolled up her mat and winked at her bestie. "What do you think? Did you like the session? How does your body feel?"

Mariah lurched to her feet. "Like my bones and joints are shouting to me they exist and they want me to pay attention to them."

"They do."

"I'm not doing this every week."

Towanda shrugged. "Suit yourself. Anytime you change your mind, come along and be my guest."

"I know you know you're not getting away with changing the subject."

"I thought I'd give it a shot."

"You missed."

"Whatever. Pick up your mat and follow me. We can walk and talk, and I'm open to your suggestions."

"Suggestions?"

"Walk and talk."

In the locker room, Mariah's frown returned with a vengeance. "All I'm saying is, after what we talked about, I'm shocked you asked him to go to Martha's Vineyard."

"Gabriel and I aren't attending alone. It's a family reunion and Nana will be there. Do you want to come too? I haven't RSVPed yet. You can bring Oscar and Binky and make it a mini-vacation on the vineyard."

Mariah flicked a blue gym towel at Towanda's arm. "Don't tempt me. You know you need a chaperone."

Towanda caught the towel and flicked it back. "Dating teenagers need chaperones. Gabriel is a friend who's coming to support me, and he knows that."

"What about you?"

"I know that too."

"Does he know about your heart?"

"I have one?"

"Stop it."

Towanda sipped her water. "Bless you. I love that you love me enough to look out for me and I'm telling you this isn't dating or the pathway into a relationship. I'm a little attracted to him, but 99% of what I feel is friendship. I love talking to him and we're good at running our business."

"What happens when the employees find out you went away together for Fourth of July weekend?"

"I'll show them the pictures of the gala and the gospel brunch and my grandmother and Lilianne and the rest of my bougie family and I'm sure Gabriel will find himself into a kitchen somewhere at midnight and show out with some late-night snack concoctions I'll take pictures of and post to Instagram."

"And all that will prove... what?"

"He came with me as a treasured colleague to deliver Philly flavor to Martha's Vineyard."

"You're sure."

"I know this."

On the drive to Mariah's home, Towanda mixed and remixed their conversation in her head. She didn't lie. No. She didn't lie at all. She'd admitted her attraction once again, but she'd also told the truth about she and Gabriel's friendship and business relationship. Talking about it was liberating. Made her feel more in control, and control was good.

If she woke in the morning and re-considered, she'd call Gabriel and use her thinkLARGE CEO voice to cancel the invitation for professional reasons. Just like Mariah recommended. Though, if she did that, she'd end up back where she started — as Nana's plus one. That would make Lilianne feel like she'd been right all along with that dumb invitation note.

Not happening. Not in this millennium.

No canceling. Gabriel and Towanda must attend the Red, White, and Blue Excellence Extravagance. She wouldn't debate herself about it any more. Tonight she'd strategize exactly how to RSVP to Lilianne, because she wanted to do it with flair.

With Gabriel right beside her.

CHAPTER 8

Gabriel

A text message banner flashed atop Gabriel's phone and the sender's name made him rush over to his office and tap the entry immediately.

Madeline Mathis. Towanda's grandmother. Also known as Nana.

> So happy you'll be our travel companion to the family reunion this July! Towanda just gave me the news. I'm having game night at my home and I just beat her in a round of chess. She's in the dining room pouting. Come over after eatLARGE closes. We'll be up late. I'll send my address.

Nana's address bubbled onto his screen along with a smiley face.

Gabriel laughed. He'd been planning to drive straight home and crash into his sleep time like the comforting promise it was after hours on his feet. But how could he say no to Nana?

He tapped the screen.

> Is midnight okay? I don't want to stop through too late. Don't want to disturb your beauty rest.

With a youthful spirit like hers, when would she ever slow down? Like grandmother like granddaughter. The Mathis women were something else. Wit, drive, and confidence. The same personality characteristics he'd love to see in his own daughters one day.

"Future family dreams," he muttered, then stepped to his doorway.

Had anyone overheard him? No. The eatLARGE staff bustled about, hard at work. So incredible how fast the team had grown. A sous chef. Part-time cooks. Full-time cooks. Servers. Hosts. Buspersons. The restaurant started as a small operation with duties that often crossed from one category to another. Now he needed everyone giving their all to their specific jobs, and he needed more than just a part-time restaurant manager for the weekends. He'd have to hire someone soon. Another task on his agenda.

Fantasizing about family life kept the stress at bay. If anyone asked him, he'd love to fill a house with girls. The more the better. Most dudes desired sons who looked and acted just like them. Not him. He'd adore being a girl dad. Three or four of them. Brown-skinned, long-legged beauties, determined to take the world by storm. The Seay girls, friends and neighbors would call them. They would float around him with grace and charm, calling him daddy and infusing his life with style and unconditional love.

If he mixed his gene pool with someone like Towanda, without a doubt, at least one of those girls would debut at New York fashion week, sporting lean builds and charm for days. The next Chanel Iman or Tyra Banks. CEO or scientist. Or a professional basketball player. He'd never limit them.

What was a man without his dreams?

A server rushed over to him. "Chef Gabriel?"

"Yes, Amari."

"Robert asked if we can turn the Closed sign on sooner than usual."

"Why?"

"Community table is at capacity and the guests at the side tables are lingering. From the looks of it, if we continue to allow more guests, we'd just have to turn them away."

Gabriel glanced at his watch. Ten-twenty. Closing time at eleven.

He nodded. "Turn the sign on, but assure our current guests we aren't rushing them to leave."

"Yes chef."

More customers equaled more receipts, but all money wasn't good money. Gabriel had learned that years ago. In a place like eatLARGE, too many bodies could impact the noise level, and complaints would increase if service slowed down. He'd stop that from happening tonight.

Besides, he had a late night meet up with Towanda and Nana.

Towanda opened the front door. Her eyes grew large. "What are you doing here?"

She'd spoken with a smile. He flashed her one in return.

"Nana invited me."

"She called you?"

"Texted me."

"This late?"

"'Bout an hour ago."

Towanda shut the heavy wooden door behind him. "You still drove over?"

"Of course."

"How come?"

"Because Nana asked." He unzipped his jacket. "She said you all would be up late, anyway."

"She ain't never lied." Towanda took his jacket and shoved sweaters and fleeces aside until space appeared in the overcrowded coat rack. "We have card games going on throughout this house, and her buddies don't tip out of here until two a.m."

He sniffed the air. Garlic. Onions. "You cooked?"

"I didn't cook anything. My life runs on grocery and meal delivery services. You are currently inhaling the rich aroma of Nana's lasagna. She's in the kitchen now." She pointed to his feet. "May I ask you to slip your shoes off, please?"

"Oh, oh yeah." He pulled them off fast, placing them next to a shoe pile.

"Thank you so much. It's not that your footwear is grubby, it's that I don't want my grandmother to spend all Saturday morning cleaning her floors, because I know she would."

He righted himself. "Got it. You said Nana's in the kitchen. Lead the way."

She grasped his arm. "Let me introduce you to the friends and fam first."

"Certainly."

A woman with class. And she looked overwhelmingly fine. He blinked three times to take it all in. Smooth midnight blue jeans and matching socks. Ivory-colored off the shoulder sweater. Curly hair up in a messy bun. She probably didn't mean it, but the way she looked? The way she touched him? Girlfriend vibes. Through and through.

"Everyone, this is Gabriel Seay. He is the creative director for eatLARGE and a friend of Nana's and mine," she announced to the poker playing crew in the living room, the serious chess players in the dining room, three older women playing Monopoly in the sun room.

"Hello. Good to meet you all." Gabriel nodded and told everyone he met.

Afterward, he grinned, strolling with Towanda to the kitchen. Bless her for introducing him, but he wouldn't remember their names. She'd rested her hand on his arm the entire time they toured the first floor. Now that, he'd remember.

"Mrs. Mathis." He spied Nana at the table, shuffling UNO cards. "So good to see you."

She rolled her eyes. "Mrs. Mathis? Oh, please. Don't show off because this is your first time here. You know you call me Nana or nothing at all. Are we clear right now?"

"Yes, ma'am."

"What would you like to drink?"

"A ginger ale, if you have it."

"Wanda, get a ginger ale for our company." She lifted her chin toward her granddaughter, then turned back to him. "Sit. Sit. You play UNO?"

He pulled out a chair and moved another out of the way to make room for his legs. "Who doesn't?"

Nana winked. "That's what I thought."

He inhaled the rich scent of homemade lasagna and garlic bread. Steamed vegetables. Apple, pecan, and strawberry pies lined up on the counter. She probably baked those this afternoon. Warm and inviting in here. Comfortable and nice. Real nice.

He accepted his soda. "Thank you... Wanda."

She stuck her tongue out at him. Slid into the kitchen chair opposite. "Don't start none. Won't be none. Understand?"

Gabriel sipped his ginger ale and laughed.

Nana dealt cards. "The only thing you need to remember for the next hour... we play stacksies in this house."

UNO and laughter and butter pecan ice cream.

Towanda complained about the sugar shock, but nothing else.

Nana played her cards and shared the Mathis family history. Roots from West Africa, then on to the tobacco farms in North Carolina and Virginia. Voice full of pride when she talked about her children, and grandchildren. She mentioned her son, Rodney, a musical prodigy, and how they'd lost him too soon. Towanda's daddy.

Towanda's eyes grew misty behind her glasses.

Gabriel reached for her hand beneath the table. He mouthed, *I'm sorry*.

She nodded and mouthed back, *thank you*.

One in the morning and Nana's eyes drifted shut. Chin on her chest, she snored while Towanda wrapped a beige fleece blanket about her shoulders.

Gabriel got up and warmed pecan pie slices for both of them.

Towanda complained again. "More sugar shock?"

"Too much for you?"

"I'll take the shock."

Blame it on the sweet pastries or the lateness of the hour, but for some reason, with every bite he watched her take, and each taste he mirrored, he felt drawn to her. Closer than before.

He stretched his long legs out beneath the table.

She did the same.

Mm-hmm. Giving him those girlfriend vibes once again.

He could get used to the feeling.

CHAPTER 9

Towanda

Towanda didn't know if Gabriel was growing tired of her showing up unannounced before eatLARGE opened for business, or after the staff shut it down for the night. If he had an issue with her sudden appearances, his face and mannerisms never displayed disgust. She understood him well enough now — if she troubled him, he would tell her the God's honest truth. He didn't play around or lie about his thoughts.

Saturday morning she used her key to open the front door and headed straight to the kitchen.

Gabriel stood in front of the stove, mixing something in a stainless steel pot. Steam billowed up, and Gabriel stared intently, his eyes focused on whatever delicious concoction he'd whipped up. Baby spinach, yeast, tapioca flour, cashews, and artichokes rested beside the cutting board.

Towanda crept closer to the stove. "Ahem."

He kept stirring. "Another moment and I'll be right with you. This needs a little more mixing and then I'll let it cool a bit."

She peered into the pot. "Spinach artichoke dip? You've made that before."

"Not quite like this. The other recipe uses sour cream, cream cheese, and butter. This one is one hundred percent vegan. No milk products."

She wrinkled her nose. "Hmm? Will it taste the same?"

"I doubt it will be exactly the same, but I'm striving to get the texture and taste close. That's why I'm testing it out." He gave the mixture another quick stir before he turned the burner off and moved the pot to a colder area of the stove. "The commenters have had their say and we need more vegan dishes."

He abandoned the stove, grabbed a kitchen towel, and wiped moisture from his large hands. He leaned against the counter and stared her up and down. "I'm surprised you're not still in your pajamas, busy sleeping in this morning, as long as we stayed with Nana last night."

"Ms. Maddie Mathis didn't outlast us, did she?"

"Not at all."

"How many UNO games did you win?"

"Can't remember."

"Me either."

A wave of self-consciousness hit her. This time she owned his full attention. Last night they were with Nana. Today she stood alone, feeling like a solitary hen strolling through a barnyard within sights of a rooster. He could make a move and she could try to fly away on useless wings, but it would be no use. She'd be prey to his will. Did she even want that?

She gazed up at him. "Thank you."

"For what?"

"For hanging out with me and Nana and her game night crew last night. You had to have been exhausted."

"I was, but I perked up when I walked in and saw—"

"Saw what?"

He moved fast to the stove. Spoon in hand, he stirred the mixture. Then he grabbed a plastic spoon, dipped it in, brought it out and tasted.

"I might need to add salt. And the texture?" He licked his lips. "Mmm. Towanda?"

"Yes."

"You gotta help me out. Taste this."

He grasped another spoon and scooped up a small bit of spinach dip, carefully bringing it to her mouth. Warmth spread across her lips.

She blew at it. "One hundred percent vegan, huh? With cashews?"

"Come on. Try it anyway," he prompted her. "Take it slow and don't burn yourself."

Towanda grasped Gabriel's hand to steady the spoon. She closed her eyes and savored, letting the flavor dance across her tongue.

Spoon still in hand, he stepped back and studied her face for a response. "So? Tell me now. Don't hold back."

A little more salt. A touch will make it perfect.

Those words formed in her mind but she had trouble making them leave her thoughts, transform into an intelligible language, and make their way into the air. All because she'd glanced away from his hand and into his huge Hershey kiss-colored eyes.

Boom. There it was. Strength combined with tenderness.

The kind she had wanted to lean into for years, but it had never materialized for her until now.

He smiled. "You can't hurt my feelings. The texture is off, right? Runny? And it needs more salt?"

She handed the spoon back and shimmied toward the kitchen door. "Uh, yeah, uh. You can... uh... try it again. But you're getting there. Another batch should do it."

"Where are you going?"

"I left my bag in my car."

"You need to get it now?"

"Yeah. My phone is inside!"

Towanda rushed across the floorboards and snatched the front door open. Fresh springtime air met her nose, and she breathed in deep. She sauntered to her, exhaling feelings blended with carbon dioxide.

Why did I come here? Why do I keep seeking him out?

She pulled her purse from the Range Rover. Hand on her phone, a notification buzzed. Chablis. God's most chipper creation had just sent a text message.

> I'm bored. I'm hungry. Bored and hungry.
> Got any healthy food down at eatLARGE?
> Perhaps some I can take home? 😊 🙏 😊

Towanda shook her head and texted back.

> Come on over, Ms. Sunshine and Rainbows.
> Help me and Gabriel test new vegan dishes.

> On my way.

"Thank you, heavenly Father," Towanda murmured. "The heat is growing, and I like this man more each day. I don't know if I'm ready. Thanks for sending me Chablis. I need her, and she needs me, too."

Last week Mariah had told Towanda that John had told Chablis he had major financial issues going on. Chablis and her parents have to foot the bill for their October wedding. Now if a man had kept that kind of secret from Towanda, she would have pawned his ring, FedExed him the cash, told him to pay his bill collectors and then propose. Hiding cash flow issues? A major deal breaker for Towanda. But Chablis seemed to have forgiven her beloved, and they were still sailing into marriage land. Good to know. Towanda had already ordered her wedding outfit: the Sachin & Babi Jacynda Optic Striped Dress from Saks Fifth Avenue.

Towanda secured her ride and turned back toward eatLARGE.

Food tasting and a deepening friendship with Chef Gabriel? So so so good. She should invite him to worship service tomorrow. Sit in the pews and praise God with him. Pray with him. Let Sunday flow and see what the Lord had in store.

CHAPTER 10

Gabriel

Gabriel had never checked himself out so much in his entire life. He'd never wanted to appear so impressive. Rise Community Church boasted a congregation of thousands, and Towanda was one of them. Before she'd left eatLARGE yesterday, she invited Gabriel to attend Sunday morning worship with her.

Of course, he'd accepted. She wasn't a *drop-in-on-holidays* type of church member — worship meant something to her. She had relationships with ladies on the women's ministry and prayer group. Whenever her friends visited the restaurant, Gabriel heard snatches of conversation about Pastor Downes, first lady Juanita, and community events the church had organized. Towanda's best friend Mariah, her husband, Oscar, and daughter, Benita. Mariah's cousin Chablis. Chablis' fiancé John. Even Gabriel's five years younger but four inches taller cousin, Michael. They all loved Rise. Gabriel preferred the simple, quieter services at Aunt Abigail's understated church.

Towanda's church invitation changed his mind. It was an offer to take part in another part of her life. No, they weren't dating, but the honey-sweet moments with her soothed his spirit. Wooed him to where thoughts of her being his employer barely entered his mind. She was simply Towanda. Smart. Striking. The one whose eyes grew large when she looked at him.

So he had no problem motoring through Philly to the elaborate gray building that took up half the block. For a big church, it had a tiny front lot. He'd skip trying to park there and leave his battered Expedition two blocks down beside a children's park.

His ride took him wherever he needed to go without a problem, even when it was constantly overdue for oil changes. Still. On the walk toward Rise, he noted every newer model BMW, Mercedes-Benz, Tesla, Cadillac and Infiniti that passed.

Don't judge these people because God is good to them. He's good to you, too. Keep it moving, man.

Gabriel quickened his steps. He ran a palm over his brushed hair. Tightened his striped tie. Made sure his pants still looked freshly steamed. Glanced down. No coffee stains on his white shirt. Towanda had asked him to meet her at the Information Desk. She would definitely be on time.

He spied her and straightened his posture. He strolled over. Checked her out in her Sunday outfit. A light-gray, button down tie-waist dress with just enough leg to display her height but keep things respectable. Gray heels and elegant silver jewelry. She sported her extra curly hairstyle today. Bushy and wild.

If this is how she looked every Sunday morning, he wanted to jump up and shout, Hallelujah!

"Can I say it?" he asked.

"Oh, you better."

"You look wonderful."

She grinned. "Thank you. You too."

She took his hand and guided him to a side hallway, away from the thick foot traffic flowing into the sanctuary. "Do you mind? I want to take a quick video of us."

"Now?"

She nodded. Gave him a sly smile. "We never sent our official RSVP to Lilianne for the Red, White, & Blue Extravaganza. You're here and we're looking amazing. We can tell her together with style."

He wrapped his arm around her shoulders. "Let's do this. Video away."

Towanda passed him her phone.

Gabriel extended it to the right angle and tapped the red record button.

She spoke. "Hello dear family! We're RSVPing direct from the City of Brotherly Love. Please add Towanda Mathis and Gabriel Seay to the attendee list—"

"Don't forget we are escorting Madeline Mathis," Gabriel's deep voice announced. "I'm looking forward to meeting you all and enjoying Martha's Vineyard with these incredible women."

Towanda waved. "See you there."

Gabriel tapped the red button to end the recording. "How did I do?"

"You're a natural." She accepted her phone back and tapped fast. "Our RSVP is on the way to my cousin."

Her smile spoke volumes when she lingered in front of him.

He followed her into the sanctuary, his heart thumping faster with each step.

Was this another girlfriend moment?

Uh-uh.

It just might be more.

Inside her beautiful Center City apartment, Gabriel lost his ability to speak.

He wandered around the living room, stammering. "This is... like gorgeous... like... I don't have the words. So... lovely."

"Thank you," she said. "Make yourself at home."

Dressed in his nicest suit, the plush living room and abstract artwork still made him want to upgrade to a better outfit. Should he sit in one of the perfect white armchairs? No. He'd wait until she told him to get comfortable. No. He'd sit. No. Stand. See what she says. Why did she invite him again? Food. Right. What was he thinking about?

Not food.

Towanda beckoned him across the large room to the kitchen island. She gestured to a high-back chair.

"I get a chance to make lunch for you for a change." She scurried to the side of the kitchen, opened a narrow door by the pantry, and pulled out a black canvas apron. "What are you in the mood for? Chicken? Shrimp? Turkey sandwiches? I have filet mignon in the back of my freezer, but I don't have time to thaw it out."

"Hold on. When I came to Nana's game night, you told me you couldn't cook."

She waggled her index finger at him. "No, no, no, my dear friend. You must have heard me wrong. I said I didn't cook. I can cook very well. Nana taught me how to make dinner for the whole family when I was eleven. When I turned fourteen I could roast a Butterball turkey, and by the time I was eighteen—"

"I get it. Point made."

Gabriel slipped his suit jacket off, draping it over the back of the chair. He took his seat and admired her kitchen. Three levels of lighting. Three-door, stainless steel, Smart Refrigerator. Hard wood flooring. White cabinets. The soft hunter green and gold striped high-backed chair he sat on. The place where Towanda brewed her morning espressos screamed class. What else had he expected?

I have to stop thinking about her needing a high-value man. I'm here because she invited me. This is my chance.

Gabriel stood on unsure legs. Words escaped his lips on their own accord. "Can I join you?"

"Excuse me?"

"Can we cook together?"

He moved to her side in seconds and quickly washed his hands at the sink. They'd left their shoes on the mat beside her front door. Without her heels on, his face hovered inches above her head. He got a faint whiff of coconut hair oil. Sweet and soft.

He asked. "You got another apron?"

Towanda jogged to the pantry and pulled out another apron. Red canvas with pink hearts.

"Here you go. Use this one." She tossed it to him.

He caught it with both hands and pulled it over his head. "You think I'm bothered by the valentine design? Ain't no issues over here, Ms. Mathis."

"Not that I had any doubt, but I receive that."

He tied the strings around his waist and whirled around, glancing here and there. None on the kitchen island. The counter? No. Maybe she stored them on a shelf in the pantry? Or inside a wire basket in one of the cabinets?

Towanda asked. "What are you searching for?"

"Onions."

"In the refrigerator."

Gabriel grabbed his chest. "Hey, no. No! Never place whole onions in a fridge unless you're trying to ruin them. Store them at room temperature. Have some respect for the food God gives us."

"Whatever you say, Chef Gabriel." She mock curtsied. "I am officially reformed."

Opening the fridge, he reached inside and pulled out a large white onion and a head of broccoli. Rummaged around and gathered minced garlic, green peppers, and top round steak. In the pantry, he claimed a jar of brown gravy and brown rice. Satisfied, he lined up everything on the counter.

Towanda crossed her arms, showing a mock pout. "What do I get to do?"

"Help me with set up. Do you have a dutch oven?"

"A what?"

"That tells me no. All right. Nana taught you to cook, so I know you have a set of cast iron skillets."

Towanda pointed to the cabinet next to his legs. "There."

Gabriel whistled when he pulled out the skillet, then stood up fast and handed her a pot. "You get to make the rice."

"Wonderful." She sauntered to the sink. Ran water. "What dish are we making?"

He pulled out her plastic cutting board. Grabbed a knife. "We're making beef and broccoli. The quick version."

He sliced and sautéed the vegetables with garlic and olive oil. She stood beside him, making the rice. He whistled. She tried to whistle his tune but failed. Started humming instead. He joined in with humming.

She put on a neo-soul music mix and they listened and sang. Cooked food and played. Stood by the stove and vibed together.

"Hey Alexa," she called to her robotic assistant. "Play Jill Scott. A Long Walk."

The electronic voice responded, "Playing "A Long Walk" by Jill Scott."

Gabriel stir-fried tenderized beef. Added it to the cooked vegetables and gravy. "You know I love this song."

"That's what you were whistling, right?"

"Um-hm. Jill sang that one to me last week."

Towanda turned up the heat beneath the rice. "Really? Where?"

"Spotify."

"Ha ha ha."

Beef and broccoli. Steaming in serving bowls, Gabriel placed the food on her dining table. Lunch was ready. They needed plates and cutlery. Wait, she was already at the buffet, pulling them out. He rushed around the table to make room for her. Back to the kitchen to wash the garlic smell from his hands. Returned to the dining area. He needed to slow down and stop looking like a fool.

She hummed "A Long Walk" while setting the solid white table with charcoal-colored ceramic plates. Curly hair wild. Apron covering her pretty outfit. Classy. Striking. Enjoying his company.

Enough of this.

"Towanda?"

She folded a napkin at his place setting. Looked up at him. "Um-hm. Did I forget something?"

He moved to her side. Licked his lips and nodded again and turned in front of her. He caught her scent. Soft. Light. Sweet. Couldn't stop his arms from pulling her close. Didn't need words when her arms wrapped around him and he felt the softness of her hands resting on the back of his head.

She purred. "This is okay?"

"This?" He kissed her lips once. Twice. Then a third time, with his heart beating so strong he could hear it.

"This is fire," he said.

CHAPTER 11

Towanda

Towanda's heart had sprouted butterfly wings. When was the last time that happened? So many years ago, the idea of pinpointing who she'd fallen for gave her a headache. Was it Jason? The guy she met at the *Black Enterprise* Entrepreneurs Conference? No. Maybe four years back with Willard. He was a community developer she'd connected with at Rise. They could have continued seeing one another if it hadn't dawned on him to move back to Tampa and "re-discover" the wife he'd left in the sunshine state.

None of that mattered. Not after she'd kissed Gabriel. Had lunch with him. Talked some more. Let him hold her and kiss her until she shooed him out the door so he could go to eatLARGE. She'd fallen into bed on Sunday night like an overly joy-filled, gawky teenager with a crush on the star high school basketball player who waved at her after each winning shot and made her feel like she was winning too.

Monday, before Jackie or anyone else, walked into thinkLARGE headquarters, Towanda paced her office. Circular path. Rectangle. Circle. She slowed each time she passed the window. Center City buses and cars and thick traffic. A metropolis awake and ready for business. People in intentional motion. Moving toward their desired destination.

She stared through the glass. Gazed at the traffic, and gripped her phone.

How could she move forward with her heart and head playing tug of war? Falling for the man who runs the restaurant she owns? Downright messy behavior. What about his heart? He'd been through so much in life. And inviting him to her condo for lunch? Really? Was she that lonely? Why had kissing him felt so marvelous? So natural. Like they'd speeded up to where they should have been all along.

Towanda rubbed her forehead. She dropped her arms and stared at her phone screen.

Dating protocol stated the man should call the morning after. Was today the morning after for two people growing closer?

She'd call him. What harm would it do?

ThinkLARGE's glass door creaked open and swung shut softly. Fluorescent lights clicked on and illuminated the front area, and footsteps across the carpet announced Jackie. Business hours would take over soon.

Towanda sprinted to her office door. She waved a fast good morning to Jackie, then closed her door for privacy.

Gabriel answered after the first ring. "Good morning, Towanda."

She smiled and held her phone close. "Good morning. It's Monday."

"Yeah, and I hate it."

"You hate your day off?"

"No, I hate that we aren't still inside Sunday. I'm thinking about those kisses."

She exhaled. "Me too."

"Sweet."

"That's one word for them."

"Surprising."

"That too."

"Succulent."

"See, now you need to stop. You sound like you're describing a dessert."

He laughed. "I'm a food guy."

Towanda strolled to the window again. "Jackie controls my calendar, so I need to check it first to make sure she didn't schedule me for something at the last minute, but I think I'm free between ten and two. Would you like to have brunch with me? I thought I'd ask because, you know, I like you, and I'd love to have some more time with you again before the workweek takes up the rest of your time and mine, and I can't believe I'm saying all this so you can stop me if— "

"Stop."

"Thank you."

"Can we turn this around? You asked me to go to the July fourth event. You asked me to church and lunch yesterday. This is getting one-sided. When do you let a brother ask you out?"

She grinned. "Forget what I said. Erase it from your mind. Go ahead, Mr. Seay."

"Appreciate it." He cleared his throat. "Ms. Mathis?"

"Yes."

"Can you check your calendar? If you are free, would you do me the honor of meeting me at Founding Farmers for brunch this morning at eleven?"

"I will check my calendar and confirm with you in a few minutes."

"Great," he said. "That's what I've been hoping for."

Without UNO cards, Towanda and Gabriel played a different game. They acted like strangers and pretended brunch was their first time sharing a meal. Ate French toast, sipped coffee, and explored each other's brains.

Gabriel asked. "How many languages do you know?"

"Spanish. French. Philly," Towanda said.

"Philly isn't a language."

"Tell that to the Webster's dictionary folks after you look up the word *jawn*." She stirred her cappuccino. "Are you an only child?"

"Yes."

"Did you like being an only child?"

"I hated it and when I have kids, I want more than three."

"I guess you want to get started right away."

"I guess so." He looked her up and down. "My turn again. Was it hard getting through Penn?"

"Not at all, except for the loneliness. Mariah went to Temple, and after she met Oscar, I lost my hanging buddy on the weekends."

"Wow. Do you have student debt?"

"No loans."

"None?"

She shook her head. "I had scholarships and grants. My grades and test scores helped. I wrote my heart out telling people about Nana raising me in south Philly, and my dad dying before I went to high school. I never met my mom — you know the story."

Gabriel gazed into her eyes. "I do."

"My turn again." She gripped her cup. "Have you dated anyone who smashed your heart and made you feel you've never gotten over her?"

He laughed. "No. Do you have a dude out there who can pop up to mess up what we have?"

"No. But what do we have, Mr. Seay?"

He took her cup and placed it on the table. Grasped both her hands. "We have the start of something extremely special."

"Extremely?"

"I'm sure you can provide a better adverb, Wharton graduate."

Towanda squeezed his hands. "Extraordinarily."

"Exclusively."

"Are you're saying that and meaning it?"

"I just did."

"Okay." She squeezed his hands again. "I receive that."

Time crept past twelve-thirty, and Towanda gathered her bag and phone. She placed her crumpled napkin and stirrer inside the empty cup. "I don't have any meetings until two o'clock, but I'd like to swing by Bloomingdale's since I'm out here. I got ink on two of my favorite work blouses last week, and I want to replace them." She stopped moving. "Thanks for asking me to brunch on your day off. This was nice."

"No need to thank me. The pleasure was all mine." Gabriel scooped her blazer from the back of her chair and helped her ease into it. "You know, if you need a shopping escort, I'm the man for the job."

"Shopping escort?"

He nodded. "Yeah."

"What if I decide I want to visit two stores?"

"My legs work."

"All right. Let's go then."

"Lead the way."

Bloomingdale's was her favorite store, so she led him there. She parked in the lot and waited until he walked over, opened her door, and helped her out.

"This feels weird." She forced herself to stand still as he shut her car door.

"What's weird about it?"

"Come on. You know. You waiting on me like this?"

He smiled and gestured for her to walk alongside him. "I've been waiting on you since we met. Every time I've put a plate of food before you, I've waited on you. The only thing different today is the car and shopping."

"You like treating women well?"

"Have you ever seen me treat anyone disrespectfully?"

"Umm... no."

"This is who I am, every day, no matter where I go."

He ushered her inside the store and stayed by her side. Halfway toward women's apparel, where the salespersons knew her by name and never followed her unless they wanted to tell her about new merchandise, Towanda stopped walking.

He asked, "Something wrong?"

"Yes." She switched her bag to the opposite arm, then slipped her hand inside his. "Now," she grasped his fingers. "This feels better. How are you feeling? Does this feel right to you?"

Gabriel shifted closer and grasped her hand tight. "If feeling like a sixteen-year-old is right." He kissed her forehead. Tugged her hand and took a step forward. "The sixteen-year-old me would tell my girl she needs to stop wasting time because we can't be out here shopping all day."

She grinned. "The sixteen-year-old me would say, all right, all right, don't rush me."

They strolled along hand in hand. People stared and smiled when they passed by. Couples who liked one another held hands. Laughed. Talked to one another in their own intimate language.

Nothing wrong with that. Nothing at all.

One Eileen Fisher System silk tank and two Lauren shirts later, and she was done shopping. She didn't need anything else except to allow Gabriel to carry her bags. She delighted in the dizzyingly, wickedly sweet, and surprising feeling of holding his firm hand as they walked along.

They passed the jewelry section, and he turned toward the Movado display. He stopped for a moment, with his eyes on the Movado Heritage Series Calendoplan Chronograph.

Towanda asked, "You like that?"

"It's cool. I'll buy it when I need another watch."

The parking lot meant goodbye. It also meant a deep kiss paired with a long, warm embrace that made Towanda want to call Jackie and cancel all the afternoon meetings. But she couldn't do that because Jackie would know she'd flipped and ever so gently suggest she hustle her butt back to thinkLARGE.

Brunch and shopping and a trip back to feeling like a teenager.

The man she adored had rested his eyes on a cool-looking Movado watch.

Hmm?

CHAPTER 12

Gabriel

Even on Gabriel's day off, he worked. Monday afternoons meant he grocery shopped for himself and Aunt Abigail. Cooked entrees and froze them for the rest of the week. Did his laundry, paid his bills, and washed and vacuumed his truck. Today was no different except he whistled his way through chores.

He'd just toured Bloomingdale's with Towanda. A stunning woman who had gripped his hand and made his emotions swell three times larger. If she didn't have to jump back into business mode this afternoon, there was no telling how the day would have gone.

Gabriel tossed a load of sheets and towels into the dryer. "I need a mature-looking life now that I might actually have somebody who wants to love me. Gotta get a respectable place of my own."

He climbed the basement stairs two at a time and ended up in Aunt Abigail's dining room. He sniffed and rushed to the kitchen. Time to turn off the heat beneath the white bean chili and move on to his next task.

Looking for an apartment.

Gabriel Seay. Poster boy for squandering free time. Not his fault, though. eatLARGE consumed 12-18 hours of his workdays. Sleep and life management scavenged his Mondays. Maybe that was why God allowed friendship and attraction to flow so freely for him and Towanda. Who else could they connect with romantically? Both of them were too busy and too grown to speed date, swipe right, or drop in on a church singles night.

He'd start with an apartment search site. See what was available and find something not too far away from the restaurant. He didn't need a big place. It shouldn't be too hard.

He typed Philadelphia into the site's search and waited with his eyes closed. Opened his eyes, and his stomach twisted. Sticker shock. Just like he'd figured. Plenty of listings, but most of them were overpriced and in gentrifying neighborhoods.

"Don't think about it, Gabe," he scrolled through listings. "You have a fine woman, and you'll find a fine apartment because she is not coming over here."

An hour of searching made Gabriel yawn and rub his dry eyes, but he'd located a decent apartment. A bi-level with two bedrooms and two bathroom and it was available. Gabriel clicked to schedule a tour. No need to waste time. Compared to the other listings, the price tag wasn't cheap, but it was reasonable.

He grabbed his phone and called Michael.

"What's up, cousin?" Michael answered.

"Aye, yo, what's good?"

"Nothing. Everything all right with mom and the house?"

"All good, but like I told you last month, I'm about to raise up out of here."

"You found an apartment?"

"I have my eye on something available. Scheduled an appointment to see it. If I go with it, can you help me move?"

"You don't even have to ask. Just tell me the day."

Gabriel smiled. "Thanks, man."

"If you need an interior decorator so you can impress Towanda, my ex-girlfriend would appreciate the business, so I can give you her number. You can see her work on the Gram at InteriorsSeventySeven."

"Hold up. What makes you think I'm trying to impress Towanda?"

"Why else would a man give up free rent?"

Gabriel nodded, phone against his ear. "Facts."

"So you want Hope's number?"

"She's your ex-girlfriend. How come you're driving business her way?"

"We were friends before we dated, and we're still friends. The love part didn't work out. I'm still her accountant. Black folk gotta support each other out here."

"True. Send me her contact after I move in."

"Cool."

"Talk to you later?"

"Talk to you, man."

Back on the site, he clicked through the pics posted to the apartment listing. New construction. Located a block and a half down from The City School, a place he'd heard about because Towanda's goddaughter, Binky, had friends who attended there and they came to her seventeenth birthday party at eatLARGE.

Towanda's life. He knew so much about it because she collected people into her universe. The business networking crowd. Her church friends. Her family. Even her financial advisor had visited eatLARGE.

What other history did she know about his life besides what Gabriel had mentioned to her when they met? His stint in jail because he'd been transparent about that when she interviewed him for eatLARGE. She knew Michael. She knew Gabriel's education and chef's experience because those were on his resume. And she knew drugs and hustling had led him to prison, but food became the passion that gave way to his future.

Why hadn't he told her more about himself or introduced her to Aunt Abigail? How come he'd never mentioned his proud Ghanian mother and how she practically abandoned him after he went to jail? Uncle Smitty, Aunt Abigail and their kids, the only committed Christians in his family. They were the only ones willing to love and support him in his new life.

How come he'd never talked about any of that with Towanda?

Because he'd grown to be a private man. He'd never shared his vulnerable stories and struggles with any employer. And until he'd kissed her, that's all she had been. An employer turned friend.

Could he even handle her knowing him at a deeper level?

When they'd walked through Bloomingdale's, heads turned. Not because they were casing the store. The salespeople called Towanda Ms. Mathis. They knew her as the head of thinkLARGE. The woman who managed the team responsible for the highly successful marketing of Mrs. Brown's Body products. Beside her, Gabriel felt like a wealthy man escorting his smart and savvy wife, and she bought her professional attire from Bloomingdale's. She'd dropped $225 on what looked like a tank top. Silk or not, it was a tank top.

And while she looked at clothes, the sales folk had been studying him. Looking him up and down while he held her hand and joked with her. They probably wondered who the heck he was. To be close with Towanda, he must be someone big in business. Was he famous? A branding expert? Or maybe a former basketball player working as a business executive for the 76ers?

No, really, who was he?

A man who bought his shoes from Foot Locker and DSW, that's who.

No one at Bloomingdale's knew his name.

Gabriel rested his back on the sofa. "Creative director. Executive chef. Chef trainer. Restaurant manager. All my titles are owned by LARGE Enterprises. Towanda's S Corp. My reality."

He leaned over his laptop. He should look at his emails. The last time he cleaned out his inbox, he had several hundred messages, and it took him more than an hour to get through them.

Not so bad. Less than sixty-five this time. Three recruitment agencies — headhunting messages intended to get him to call or email and ask for more information about a "popular restaurant" seeking Gabriel's extraordinary talents for creative cuisine, even temperament, leadership skill, willingness to educate, and effective communication. Not Gabriel's words — theirs. He used to see messages like these once a season. This year he'd seen an average of ten each month. One recruiter had gotten bold, somehow gotten his cell phone number, and started calling him. He'd blocked the number and double-checked to make sure his resume wasn't appearing on any career-related sites.

Towanda hired him to make eatLARGE successful, and she'd taken all the risk on herself.

He'd never sell out and hop to another restaurant, even if they could pay him more.

Money wasn't everything.

Gabriel spied the box as soon as he opened eatLARGE. A small white cardboard package with a red satin bow. It sat at the edge of the bar. The note on top read: *Please Open Me.*

He glanced around. Was he alone? He had to be. Emptiness surrounded him.

"Hello," he called out and picked up the box. "Who put this here?"

Nothing.

He let his bag slide to the floor. "I don't like surprises," he called to the air. "If a crowd of y'all are in the back waiting to jump out and yell happy birthday, you're over three months early. I'm an August baby. Leo in the house."

Nothing.

Gabriel shook the box. Turned it around. Shook it again. "I'm about to open this. Again, I don't like surprises. You've been warned."

He took the box with him to the kitchen. Flipped on the lights and peered around. Empty.

"Got me in here talking to the air," he muttered. "Might as well open it."

He ripped open the packaging and let the cardboard and bow drop to the floor. Brown paper shreds fell when he lifted out another box. A watch box.

Movado.

He lifted the top and gazed at the arm jewelry. The Movado Heritage Series Calendoplan Chronograph. The same one he'd stared at during the Bloomingdale's trip. Only Towanda had seen him look at it, so the watch must have come from her.

He put the watch down and backed away. He touched his chest, then his face, trying to rub away the sinking feeling that gripped him.

He clenched his fists. Unclenched them. Clenched them again. Wanted to push himself past uncomfortableness and failed.

Why didn't he buy the watch himself? Because he couldn't afford to drop a little over a grand on a brand new watch. Not without some planning, and even then, he wouldn't do it because he needed to spend his money on other things, like a new apartment and a later model truck.

Towanda probably figured it would be expedient to handle the issue and buy the Movado. She could afford it, and that was proof they were not in the same league, unless running their establishment or kissing.

Gabriel stumble-stepped to his bag and pulled out his phone so fast he almost dropped it. Tapped her name in the contacts before he knew what to say.

He spoke to her voice mailbox. "Ms. Mathis, I got the watch. I'm leaving it untouched so you can return it to Bloomingdale's with no problems. I'm sure you meant well, but I'm not taking it. That's all I have to say. Thank you."

CHAPTER 13

Towanda

Towanda had been wrong. She'd considered the date and the time — the two most essential elements of the plan. She'd calculated and recalculated the exact strategy for days, and she still failed.

She'd walked into eatLARGE close to midnight that Friday, she found Gabriel.

She also found the sous chef, servers, cooks, and hosts seated at the community table with him.

She took in the sight of them all under the dim lighting. She would have willed her feet to take her in the opposite direction, except they turned around fast. Silent. Eyebrows raised with the same question on their faces. *What's she doing here?*

Gabriel pushed his chair back and stood. "We're all tired, but I'm sure everyone remembers their training. Our establishment owner is here." He clasped his hands before him. Gave a quick nod. "Ms. Mathis, good evening to you."

"Good evening…"

"Hello…"

"Hi, Ms. Mathis."

"Hey, Ms. Mathis."

"Good evening…"

"Hi…"

Gabriel narrowed his eyes. "Now then, Ms. Mathis, how can we help you? Are you stopping through to check on us? We're doing quite well, and if you want to stroll through to the kitchen, you'll find everything in pristine condition."

Towanda's stomach lurched, but she planted her feet firmly on the hardwood floors. She squinted at him. Who in the world was this? Not the sweet man who kissed her last week? It couldn't be the caring guy who'd helped wrap a blanket around her Nana after playing endless UNO games. What happened to the gentleman who sang with her from the church hymnal and helped make lunch at her condo afterward?

He'd been replaced by an overgrown clown who glared at her like she was an intruder in her own restaurant. Because of a gift? Was he serious?

New Gabriel? Time to meet old Towanda. No-nonsense, boss babe, *don't-come-for-me-or-I'll-rip-you-to-shreds-and-ask-God-for-forgiveness-later,* Towanda.

She stepped further into the dining area. Undid the buttons on her trench coat slowly. "Good evening, staff. It's wonderful to see all of you, especially at such a late hour. Chef Gabriel doesn't normally keep you past midnight, does he?"

Antonio raised his hand. "No. Not at all. He never overworks us."

"Excellent. I'd hate to receive a negative report about him. Your opinions count, and you all are the heart and soul of this restaurant." Towanda placed her coat on a wall hook. She walked over toward Gabriel, stopping a yard's distance from him. "Like Chef Gabriel inferred, eatLARGE is a family, and we want to treat each other with respect and tender care."

He huffed. "You know I don't overwork anyone."

She crossed her arms and glared. "Do I?"

"You do."

"Really? Because I thought I knew a lot of things. I was wrong."

Was that smoke coming out of his ears? Wow! That happened fast. His first time facing off with old Towanda, they hadn't even said the word *watch*. If they kept trading anger lines in front of an audience, he'd probably self-combust.

Gabriel shuffled back and faced his staff. "Thank you for an amazing night. Everyone, please get home safe. Tomorrow will be another busy day."

Antonio raised his hand. "But Chef Gabriel—"

"We'll continue our meeting tomorrow. Good night." Gabriel directed his body toward the kitchen.

"Good night, everyone," Towanda parroted. "As Chef Gabriel said, please get home safe."

Gabriel stood silhouetted in the doorway. "Ms. Mathis?"

"Mr. Seay?"

"Can you join me in the kitchen, please?"

She pivoted around. Half the staff was out the door. The other half were poised to walk out behind them.

"Towanda?"

"Hold on!"

Five. Four. Three. Two. One. The door shut. She hurried to the front and locked it securely. Moved to the wall switch and shut off the lights. Slowed her gait on the way to the kitchen. Took her time. He'd left her that ungrateful voice mail then said nothing else to her for the rest of the week. Let him simmer.

She figured he'd be pacing kitchen floor, arms crossed, sweat on his brow, ready to fire back at her.

Wrong again.

He sat on a stool and gestured to the one across from him.

She asked, "I'm supposed to sit there?"

"What do you think?"

"You don't have to sound so nasty."

He swept his large hand toward the stool again. "You're right. Please. Have a seat."

She sat and studied his tired eyes and drooping mouth. Listened to the sound of their breathing. At least they were in sync in that capacity. All of this because of a timepiece?

Towanda laced her fingers together and placed them on her lap. "Where is it?"

"Locked in my desk drawer."

She sniffed. "The way you sounded on the voice mail, I'm surprised you didn't drop the box in the garbage and pile rancid raw salmon on top of it after I failed to come to pick it up. Seeing how having it upset you so darn bad."

Gabriel raised his hands. "Towanda Mathis. We. Are. Not. Doing. This. We are professionals. Please."

"Professionals?"

"Yes."

She tapped her toe against the tile. As much as it bugged her, he was right. They should have remained in professional mode, and they failed right in front of the eatLARGE staff members. It was wrong and Towanda knew better. Now both of them probably had the entire staff gossiping, and it had nothing to do with them falling for each other.

Ridiculous.

"Gabriel?"

"Yes."

"It was a watch."

He shook his head. "It's a watch to you, but to me it means something. You are never, ever, paying for anything for me again."

"Are you serious? You're turning a gift into some man versus woman power trip?"

"Call it what you want, but the Movado was something I wanted for myself. I pay for the things I want and need. I don't need you to do it for me."

"This conversation is silly." She stopped tapping her foot. "Last week we sent Chablis home with three nights' worth of healthy dinners she could share with John. When Binky had her birthday party, you saw the diamond necklace I got her. Friends give each other gifts because they're friends. I didn't buy it for you because you couldn't get it yourself, and I didn't start falling for you because of anything involving money. I like you for you. If I want to pursue men who have big money, I can... "

She halted the words escaping her mouth. Hit the pause button because Gabriel's eyes were growing larger. Sweat beads glistened on his forehead two beats after she'd uttered *men who have big money*.

"Oh, no. Go on! Don't stop now. Tell me how you feel, Ms. Mathis." He raised an eyebrow and leaned toward her. "What are you saying about men with big money?

She gazed at floor tiles and mumbled, "Nothing. That has nothing to do with this conversation."

He got up, stayed gone for a minute, returned to her side with the watch box in hand.

He handed it to her. "Here you go."

She clutched it. "I don't know what to say."

"I do." He backed away. "I don't know if I'm the type of man you need."

She stood, still grasping the box. "Who said I needed a man at all?"

"Pardon?"

"We've been having a great time, and mostly, it feels like heaven on earth. But I've never said that I *needed* a man. That's some last century mess I've never subscribed to. I am fine and I've always been fine without one. "

Gabriel sniffed. "Hey. Okay. I stand corrected. You didn't need a man. You asked for a plus one. A friendly escort. If that's all I am, then I need to stay in my lane."

It took less than an hour for Towanda to confront Gabriel about his attitude about the watch, and less than a minute for them to be at odds with one another. Distant and throwing bitter words like ice cubes. She couldn't say anything else to him. If she did, she'd probably make things worse.

She headed toward the doorway. Called over her shoulder, "Goodnight."

"'Night."

CHAPTER 14

Gabriel

"What do you think?" Gabriel stepped through the white-walled apartment space. Admired the gleaming hardwood floors and the wide windows. "This is the spot for me?"

Michael glanced up from his phone. Gazed around. "You need this much room, though? Two floors and two bedrooms? I mean, it is just you. Unless you have kids we don't know about."

"No, man. I'm never doing the whole baby mama thing."

"Just checking. You're more popular by the day. I see all those ladies putting comments and hearts on your IG posts. Some of them are kind of cute."

"Those women are liking meals, not me. They're looking for celebrity chefs for their glamorous events." He slid open the hall closet. Clean and roomy. "I can't get anybody pregnant with spicy mango ginger soup."

"If you can, you have to teach me your secret."

"Man, shut up."

Gabriel stepped into the bathroom and frowned. The natural stone and earth brown colors. Those were fine. But the room itself was kind of small. Could he even shower here comfortably? Surprising for an apartment with so much room in it. He'd bet the downstairs bathroom had the same problem.

"Mike?"

"Yeah."

"Run downstairs and let me know what that other bathroom feels like to you? This one is smaller than I thought. From the pictures, I thought it would be bigger."

Gabriel leaned against the pedestal sink. It didn't rock. He bent down and tried to jiggle the toilet. It didn't budge. Good. The bathroom was smaller than he'd thought, but at least it had solid workmanship. He could use it day after day and not worry about breaking anything and having to call the landlord and wait for repairs. Gabriel didn't have time for all that.

Michael loomed in the doorway. "Yo, that bathroom is *niiiice*. You know, I could live here. You want a roommate?"

"What are you talking about? You're not moving back to the city trying to pay Philly wage tax." Gabriel brushed past his cousin and moved to the staircase.

Michael trailed him. "I'm saying though, this could be our bachelor pad if we put a little swag on it. I wouldn't mind saving on housing costs. I could put more in my investment accounts each month and start dabbling in bitcoin."

"For real? Then how come you moved out of your mom's house? Aunt Abigail would have let you stay there as long as you wanted."

"Because—"

"Let me finish for you. Because you didn't want to be a black man in your late twenties living with your mama and have to explain that to Hope or anyone else you tried to go out with."

"Ouch."

"Mm-hm. And I'm too old to have a bachelor pad. I'm just trying to live."

Gabriel turned onto the bottom floor. The upstairs primary bedroom was larger than the one down here, and it was close to the kitchen. He envisioned himself staying up there. The bathroom down here could make him change his mind. "Whoa."

Michael nodded. "Told ya."

This must have been the bathroom he saw in the online virtual tour. Nearly twice the size of the upstairs bathroom and it had the larger tub with jets, double sink, exposed brick on one wall, and two lighting levels. He could play his music and relax in here, soaking his body and releasing stress after hours on his feet.

Gabriel circled around once. "This is it."

"Nice right?"

"No doubt."

"You think Towanda might like it?"

Gabriel cleared his throat. "It doesn't matter because she won't see it."

"What happened? At church you were holding her hymnal and singing along with her. Did she hit the wrong notes?"

"Something like that."

"She got another man?"

"Not that I know of." Gabriel took out his phone. He'd call the rental agent and let him know they were done checking things out. He could get the paperwork and sign on the dotted line for the apartment. "And if she did, hurray for her. I'm not the man for her, anyway. I knew that before."

Michael stopped him from dialing. "Wait. Did she tell you that?"

"No, but I know."

"How?"

"We went shopping."

"What's wrong with that?"

"And she bought me a watch."

"Again. What's the problem?"

Gabriel sighed. Stopped looking at his phone screen. "Towanda Mathis is out of my league. She's the type of woman who salespeople know by name when she steps into Bloomingdale's buying a shirt. She buys diamonds for her goddaughter. Her family holds reunions on Martha's Vineyard. She's a cool person to know, but I'm not in her ballpark for love, and I'm not trying. We're falling back to friend status, and I'm going to ask her to stop dropping by the restaurant unannounced."

"But it's her restaurant."

"I do the job of several people and LARGE Enterprises pays me to orchestrate everything happening inside eatLARGE. I shouldn't have been at church with her or anyplace else that didn't have to do with food or business. It was my fault for getting caught up. It's not gonna happen again."

Michael shook his head. "Oh, look at you, handsome rising chef, feeling sorry for yourself for no reason."

"Man, shut up."

What was Mariah doing at eatLARGE early on a Thursday?

Gabriel unlocked the front door. "Hey, Mariah. What's going on?"

"Hey, Gabriel." She stepped inside. "I wanted to stop through for a minute. Just to talk to you. Can we sit?"

"Oh yeah. Sure." Gabriel snapped out of his trance and led Mariah to the community table. He pulled out her chair.

"Thanks," she said.

Mariah was a beautiful woman, but seeing her made his stomach sink like a rock. He'd been doing a great job blocking all thoughts of Towanda. No calls or texts to her. They needed the breathing space, and the staff needed time to forget what they'd experienced. This morning he'd greeted the day with a peaceful, calm feeling. Now here was Mariah staring him in the face, destroying blissful ignorance about Towanda.

His heart beat a little faster in his chest. He would ignore the sensation. Pretend to be fine. Remain strong and cool. Act like he didn't miss her.

Gabriel offered Mariah his gentleman smile. "What do you want to talk about?"

"I want to tell you about Towanda."

"Do you need something from her?"

Mariah frowned. "Besides Nana, I'm the only other person with keys and codes to her condo. If I needed something from her, I can pick it up myself. That's not why I'm here."

He crossed his arms. Whether or not he wanted to hear about Towanda, he was going to. "Go on. Is she okay?"

"She's a mess."

"Really? I'm sure she's still running things like a boss."

Mariah shook her head. "You don't understand. Whenever she's uncomfortable with something, she works herself into the ground so she can distract herself from the pain. It's her coping mechanism. She's taking part in a panel discussion at the Rise leadership retreat. She's booked as a speaker at an entrepreneur's conference next week. She's also modeling for Mrs. Brown's Body's new natural makeup line, and she's on a podcast tour she doesn't even have time for."

"Jackie lets you peek at Towanda's calendar?"

"Sometimes. Gabriel? What happened?"

"She hasn't said anything to you?"

"Said anything about what?"

"Brunch. Shopping. The watch. Nothing?"

"No. What watch?"

Gabriel rolled his eyes. "She bought me the Movado I wanted, and I told her to take it back and that made her mad, so she came over here and both of us play-acted crazy right in front of our staff."

"You're joking."

"No, I'm not."

"That's not like her."

"Not like me either."

Mariah looked up and searched Gabriel's face. "I think she's in love."

Love? The word hit his ears and slithered into his body slowly. His heart beat double time again. In love? With him? A dude who bought his clothes without customized help from a snooty salesperson?

Gabriel shook his head. "Love? She loses control and spits out words like venom when she's in love? What does she do when someone truly troubles her?"

Mariah shuddered. "You don't want to know. Even talking about it will give me flashbacks."

"Oh? Really?"

"We're over that now, and she's changed. She can be the sweetest person on earth when she loves you, and she's extremely generous. So…" Mariah pointed to his empty wrist. "She gave you a watch. When you wouldn't take it, it's like you told her you don't like her. She can handle that from anyone except you."

He shifted around, faced the front door, and rested his hands on his knees. He hadn't thought. Hadn't considered. The Movado hadn't been a charity move or a manipulation tactic. Towanda was only behaving like her generous self. Mariah. Binky. Chablis. All of them were used to Towanda's ability to give unconditionally.

He'd come face to face with Towanda's love gesture, and he dodged it. Because he thought she was taking care of what she knew he couldn't.

Gabriel rubbed his hands together and muttered, "Sugar. Honey. Iced. Tea."

"What—"

"You're a churchgoing lady. I'll spare you, okay?"

"Thanks."

He turned back to Mariah. "Listen, Towanda is my friend above everything else, and I'll talk to her soon, I promise. Thanks for letting me know what's going on with her."

"She would do the same thing for me. And I have one other thing I want to talk about."

"Okay?

"Can you bring me on as a full-time restaurant manager?"

"You actually want all those hours?"

"I've thought about the position since Towanda told me she was starting this place. I wasn't ready then, though." She shrugged. "Part-time works well for me, but I can do more. Binky drives now. She's going to college soon, and Oscar would be more comfortable if I stay at work with a business he's acquainted with. Around people he knows."

Gabriel tapped his foot. "You asked at the right time. Give me a day or two and I'll get back to you. All right?"

She nodded and gave him a mock salute before she left.

He shook his head. Mariah. Nana. Being in Towanda's world meant he had to accept the truth: she wasn't the only bold person in her camp.

Mariah would take a huge load of work off his shoulders. Plus she was smart, old enough for the staff to respect her, and young enough to relate to them. Gabriel would hire her to come on board full-time. It would give him a chance to move forward on a high note. He still wasn't the man of elevated status Towanda deserved, but he could be a gracious friend. His heart? Hopefully God would give it a second chance with whomever was right for him.

CHAPTER 15
Towanda

Towanda and Mariah walked through the late spring air, circling the block around Mariah's home. With Binky and Oscar in the house, this was the only way they could have a private conversation.

"Friend?" Towanda asked.

"That's what he said?" Mariah pumped her arms while she walked. "That's good."

"That's...terrible." Towanda frowned. "*Friend*? Did he add the word *zone*? Let me unpack what you said. Did he say friends like friends like we're all friends, or was he talking about me specifically as a friend, like all he wants me to be is a friend?"

"How many times can you put friends in a sentence? The man said friends, I took it that your friendship is important to him, so I shared it with you, and now you want me to analyze how he said it?"

"Please?"

"No." Mariah took off faster.

Towanda jogged to catch up. She'd stay in lockstep and keep talking. "Okay, no analysis. Just give me an idea of how he looked."

"Disturbed."

"Disturbed?"

"I thought the whole time he was going to tower over me and expose that you sent me down there on a peace mission."

"But he didn't, so it's cool."

Mariah tsked. "Listen, don't send me to do your dirty work again. I don't enjoy lying to people."

"You didn't lie. You didn't know about the Movado."

"No, I didn't. Why didn't you tell me?"

"The watch thing didn't end well. You told me you were going down there to talk about a full-time position. I figured you could piggyback issues and tell him how I'm doing."

Mariah stopped and stood in front of her. "You're slipping back to behavior you repented from. Don't do it with me and don't do it with Gabriel. It's not fair to us."

Towanda examined the white laces in her Adidas sneakers. "You're right. I apologize." She raised her head and Mariah's eyes. "Manipulation isn't the move, I get it. But I don't know what else to do."

"You like him that much?"

"I do."

"Stop pushing so hard and learn more about him. If you follow God's lead, as time passes, trust me, if Gabriel is the man for you, he'll be right there."

"That's easy for you to say. You're married to a loyal husband. You raise a kid with him. You enjoy a secure relationship. You aren't in your mid-thirties praying for love." Towanda wrapped her arms around herself and rubbed her own back. "I get distracted and lonely sometimes. Sometimes I want to be held and kissed and—"

Mariah's eyes lit up. "Kissed?"

"Let's stay on topic."

"Ahem. Kissed?"

"I said held too."

"Back to kissed."

"It's not a big deal."

"More than kissing? No. Uh-uh. If you'd done more, you would have told me. But you didn't tell me about the watch, either." Mariah's eyes grew larger. "Did you do more than kiss?"

"No. We're not ready for all that."

"If you did, you're an adult. You're only accountable to God."

"I'm accountable to God and myself. Double accountability. Waking up in the morning with no commitment from a man who works for my corporation? Um... no ma'am."

Towanda looked up the hill. Mariah's house waited at the top. They would get there and she'd eat dinner and dessert with Mariah, and Oscar, and Binky. Relish their company and their sense of family.

Later tonight her empty condo would wait for her, along with an overdue task she didn't want, but she must handle.

Towanda swiveled around in her home office chair. She tapped her phone for voice mail and played the message. The fourth time today.

"Good day, attendees." Imani, Lilianne's chirpy personal assistant, addressed through automated message. "Since we are approaching the one month mark before the Red, White, and Blue Extravaganza, we want to touch base with you personally. Please shop ahead of time for your color-coordinated outfits. Remember that linen is perfect for the weather on the Vineyard. Also, be sure to double check your transportation plans. Last, please call and re-confirm your RSVP. We understand that life happens. If your plans changed, give us the courtesy of knowing before the reunion weekend. We will communicate with the hotel regarding your room or suite booking. We look forward to seeing you all. Be well."

Towanda tapped to stop the playback. If Lilianne was suddenly cast as the next member of *The Real Housewives of Potomac*, Towanda wouldn't be surprised. The chick sure knew how to put pressure on people to ensure she managed a near perfect family event.

Towanda tilted her face toward the ceiling and counted ceiling fan revolutions. Lilianne. *That* cousin. The one with the perfect suburban parents, pampered upbringing, and every reason to look down her snooty little nose at Towanda.

But she had already bought her outfits, and her travel bags were practically packed. She wouldn't have to check with Nana. Nana was the original travel gangster. She stayed ready and owned every outfit she'd ever need, in all the colors of the rainbow.

Gabriel.

If Mariah's guidance was correct, and why wouldn't it be, Towanda shouldn't use him as a plus one. She'd have to be strong enough to admit the truth: she was in heavy "mutual like" with a friend. Current status equaled complicated.

Translation? Single. Incurably, no. Single, yes.

She shouldn't have asked him to attend. If she cancelled his RSVP, they could return to normal. Pretend she never asked. She should never have let her guard down with him anyway, personally or professionally.

Towanda tapped for speaker phone mode and delivered her return message to Imani. "Hello, this is Towanda Mathis. I am returning your call regarding the Red, White, and Blue Extravaganza. Final RSVP and hotel confirmation for Towanda Mathis...and Madeline Mathis."

CHAPTER 16
Gabriel

Gabriel rolled over, opened his eyes, and jumped. His phone buzzed and danced beside him on the bed and there was her picture, showing she was calling him.

Towanda.

He reached over and snatched up the phone, knocking two pillows to the floor. "Gabriel Seay."

"Towanda Mathis."

"What time is it?"

"Early."

He scrambled to a sitting position, rubbed the sleep from his eyes. Pulled the phone away from his ear, and glanced at the screen. "You're calling me at five forty-five in the morning? Did eatLARGE burn down overnight?"

"It better not have."

"Okay." He pulled the phone away again and yawned into his fist. Only God and Towanda were up and fully functional at this hour. "Question? How early do you normally get up?"

"Around four-thirty. Sometimes at four, depending. Are you awake? Can you talk?"

This woman. She hadn't spoken to him in a week and a half and now she wanted him alert and bantering before the sun woke up this side of the world. The only way he wanted to engage with her at this hour was if she wore his ring and was cuddled in his arms beneath silky sheets and a thick comforter.

And that wasn't happening.

"I'm awake." He tapped the speakerphone icon. "What's going on?"

Her voice echoed in the dark. "Yes, well, I don't want to waste time. First, thank you for agreeing to be my plus one for the family reunion."

"You're welcome—"

"But, because of current circumstances, I've changed my mind. Nana and I will attend on our own. I confirmed with Lilianne's assistant last night. Thank you, again, for agreeing to accommodate us."

Cancelled. This woman...this grown woman. Just cancelled him.

He stared at his phone.

"Gabriel?"

"Towanda."

"Did you—"

"I heard you." He shook his head. Rubbed at the goosebumps on his bare arms. "What do you want me to say? Thank you for using and confusing me?"

She paused. "I think it's better this way."

"I'm sure you do."

"Do you have questions?"

Early hour. Crisp voice. All business. Yeah. Okay. She was playing the role of the CEO. Back in her box of being the friendly boss. All right. She could do that. Darned if he would stop her.

He had a choice, too. His choice was to drop into the safety zone where business interests were all they shared. Love was too dangerous.

He said, "No questions. But I have a request for you."

"Go ahead."

"Can you please announce when you plan to visit eatLARGE? Allow me and the eatLARGE team the courtesy of being at our best before you arrive? Can you do that for us?"

She paused. "Absolutely."

"Good. Have a fabulous day."

"Good day."

Gabriel stared at his phone until the light turned off. He slid it onto the nightstand, and himself back beneath the bedcovers. A blanketed cocoon in a dark room and he was wide awake and feeling too much. Yes, the call ended cordially, but he still rubbed the center of his chest like he could calm his heart.

Broken-hearted? How do you break up with someone you weren't truly dating? What did he and Towanda actually have together? A business and a friendship that grew out of that business. Church. Lunch. Kisses. Shopping. More kisses. And the only thing that remained the same throughout all that was the business. His role at eatLARGE never changed. One thing that remained the same and five events that didn't amount to anything.

Gabriel shivered. He closed his eyes and burrowed deeper beneath the covers.

He whispered, "God, I should pray more. I'm praying now because I shouldn't be hurt by her decision, but I am. Comfort my heart, Lord, because I hate this feeling. I hate it."

He relaxed and drifted into the dimmed brightness between awake and asleep. Pictured himself in a different time and space. Twenty-two-year-old Gabriel in prison. Laying on his side at night in the dark, bitter and empty about calls his father wouldn't accept, and letters his mother wouldn't send. Alone. Not religious, but grasping the idea that God might be his only genuine friend. Gabriel toiling in the kitchen and serving the inmates. The cool big dude who poured his heart and soul into meager ingredients and invented meals that made people cheer. He did it again and again. Did what he could do and learned to do more.

Moved from punished and alone to confident, diligent, and skilled.

More was in store for him beyond current hurt and confusion.

Towanda drifted into his inner visions. Interview day Towanda. Welcoming him into empty restaurant space for eatLARGE. She'd jolted him then, but not because of physical attraction. Because he'd never seen a woman be so loving while strategized to accept so much risk. She'd brought her goddaughter with her while she interviewed chefs for a new restaurant and she had no idea if the concept would work. She'd smiled at him. Listened to his story. Tasted one bite of his food, hired him, put him in the driver's seat and let him shine. Had her corporation pay him before the first customer ever walked through the eatLARGE doors.

He would never serve her another late night mushroom chicken dinner. No special meals whipped up at her condo. He'd never hold her or kiss her again. He needed to slaughter every fantasy about their future.

He'd have to eat his conflicting emotions for breakfast, digest them before lunch, and force himself to present a satisfied smile.

Towanda

Towanda cranked up the car air conditioner so she wouldn't have sweat stains on her white blouse, or "glow" through her makeup. Sunshine streamed through the windshield. When had mid-June been so hot? If Philly temps registered in the nineties without even a little relief from the wind, what would July feel like? The first level of hell?

Mariah whimpered. "Are you trying to freeze me?"

"I'll turn down the air. My goodness, you can't take a little cold?"

"Cool air doesn't bother me. Frigid air does."

"Why do you keep checking yourself out in the mirror?"

"I don't know. Being full-time staff gives me a different vibe. I'm not just lending a hand anymore, I have a title."

"Well, you look beautiful, competent, and confident."

Mariah flipped the passenger side visor back up. "Thank you. Binky did my makeup."

"You're living with your own personal makeup artist. I'm jealous. I hope she used the Mrs. Brown's Body products I gave her."

"Why?"

Towanda turned left off Broad Street. "I believe in the thinkLARGE clients, and I want us to support them. When they do well, we all do well. Binky loves her necklace?"

"You know she does."

Towanda eased off the gas and scanned the street for a parking spot. "Then tell her to make sure you're a walking billboard for Mrs. Brown's Body whenever she does your face." She frowned. "Can't park on the side like I usually do. Um. I won't be here long. I'll park in front."

"Sidewalk."

"Yep."

"Aren't you risking a ticket?"

"I'm not staying long and I'm not going inside."

Towanda drove across the curb, parking the Range Rover as close to eatLARGE as she could. She eyeballed the space and left just enough to open the driver's side door. She put the flashers on.

Mariah grabbed her bag from the back seat. "I appreciate you being my personal chauffeur. Now why you aren't going in?"

"I didn't make the time to call first to let anyone know I'd be here. Don't want to upset the staff or anything like that." She sighed. "Gabriel and I agreed I wouldn't show up to the restaurant unannounced, so I'm not. I am outside, in my own car, parked on the sidewalk."

"T? You're both nuts. You should stop being passive aggressive with one another and treat each other with compassion."

"Gabriel runs eatLARGE and I'm staying out of his way. Today, I'm here to support you."

Mariah hugged her and gave her a quick back rub. Released her. "He'd be fine if you walked in to say hello."

"If I see him, I'll wave at him through the glass."

"Silent owner to the extreme."

"We'll talk again. He's free to call me if he has any issues with our accountant, payroll, sales and marketing, or any of our agreed upon standard operating procedures."

"Seriously, you aren't coming in?"

"I don't have to check on anything. He's beyond competent at every task with this restaurant, including hiring the right employees." Towanda sighed. "Even if we hadn't hit a speed bump, he wouldn't need me here."

Mariah touched her door handle. "What about Chablis' bachelorette party?"

"It's June. The party is in September. Plenty of time for you to plan a celebration as glam as the woman it's for. You're the party pro. Tell me how much to contribute."

"My party skills are stellar. I want to make sure you're here for it."

"I'm not missing my chance to send Ms. Sunshine and Rainbows off in style. I'll be sitting right next to Nana, in the big comfy chair."

"Good."

Towanda grinned. "Now get out. You're going to be late."

"I don't do late. I'm out."

Towanda got out of the car. Stretched her legs and watched her bestie skip up the stairs to eatLARGE, like she was sending a daughter off to high school. Not that she'd had the experience, but she could imagine.

The glass door swung shut, and Towanda almost put herself back inside the car.

Almost.

Gabriel appeared behind the glass. Tall and handsome. Confident and strong and staring at her. He waved.

She wanted to wave back. Tried to lift her hand but her fingers wouldn't move. She froze and blinked and sweat trickled down her cheek but wouldn't let herself wipe it away with a tissue. Her heart hammered inside her chest, and her mouth went dry.

He nodded slowly.

She nodded back and gave him thumbs up like *thank you for hiring my bestie... good move.*

She caught his half-smile, another short wave and a nod, then he turned and walked away so fast it seemed the dim dining room swallowed his body.

Heart still hammering, she waited. Sweated and shifted her weight while looking through the glass door and envisioning him pushing it open. Couldn't he open the door and his heart, jog down those stairs and speak the words necessary to erase all the negative feelings between them?

Minutes passed with the day's heat beating down on her.

Towanda and Gabriel. All the good feelings gone.

Towanda's nerves twitched and telegraphed anxious messages across too many brain pathways.

Get back in the car. Drive. Don't look for him. Don't return here unless an emergency occurs. Whatever was precious between you two, it's gone. Dead. His eyes had confirmed that.

Driving back to Broad Street, she grumbled, "Congratulations, Wharton grad. You built a lucrative business, then killed a beautiful friendship."

CHAPTER 18

Gabriel

Gabriel had just stepped out of his office when Antonio rushed to him.

"Chef Gabriel?"

"Yes, Antonio."

"A man walked in and asked to speak with you personally."

"Who is it?"

"Bearded guy who looks like he should own a gym. Says his name is John."

"Yeah, John." Gabriel glanced at his watch fast, then back to Antonio. "Let me see what this is about. I want you to keep everything running smoothly in the back of the house. No shortcuts, and all meals must be expertly plated and served on time. I'm counting on you."

Antonio beamed a gap-toothed smile. Straightened his posture. "Yes, Chef Gabriel."

Antonio was turning out to be one of eatLARGE's best employees. On time daily. Always ready to go beyond the call of duty as a sous chef. The cooks and servers respected him. Antonio's past drug and gang activity and his short jail sentence hadn't derailed him from starting over and learning a new trade after his release from prison. It made Gabriel proud to have hired and invested in the young man.

Every man deserved a good start to a transformed life.

Gabriel headed to the front. He walked over to John and they traded the classic Philly half pound, half hug greeting. "What's up, man? How're you doing?"

"Good. Good. How's business?"

"Busier each week." Gabriel leaned against the bar. "Last two weekends we had lines out the front door. Surprised you rolled through. Thought the new fiancée would soak up all your free time. How's she doing?"

"She's fine. You know Chablis. Even a bad day is a good day for her."

"I know, right?"

John lifted his chin. "Actually, she's the reason I'm here. We've been working through money issues, and other stuff... some of its bananas, but whatever... I'll keep it short... we're fast tracking it to the wedding, but this isn't the engagement period the wifey expected."

"Okay?"

"Every day she tells me she loves me. Like two or three times a day. She's still down for me and that means something. I want to do something grand for her, and I might need your help."

"You want a surprise here at the restaurant? Shut the place down? Have a private romantic dinner with her?"

"Nah, I want something bigger."

"What?"

"I'm not sure yet, but it'll involve some catering, and your food is the best. Chablis and I are working with wedding planners and they understand our situation. Would you mind if I have them call you? They're better at this type of thing than I am. If you and Towanda and the eatLARGE crew can pitch in with the surprise, Chablis would love it. If you can't swing it, no worries. It's all good."

"No problem. You got it."

"Thanks, man."

"You mind answering a question for me?"

John nodded. "Sure."

"You said Chablis is down for you, even with the financial issues. She's not trying to walk out?"

"Crazy, right? She is definitely, one hundred percent my life partner.

We're only waiting on the vows to make it official, but we've been a team since we first got together. She cares about where we're headed in life, not where we are today, and two can always do better than one. We have our dreams and we'll build together."

Dreams. Building together. Marvelous stuff. Gabriel and Towanda had experienced the same thing when they met. Right after she'd hired him and they'd spent weeks planning and transforming the restaurant space. They'd kicked up dust together. Reviewed blueprints for the interior. She'd approved every idea he had for the kitchen design and dining room. Deferred to him for everything eatLARGE related. Like eatLARGE was their baby. A creative conception, and the food and the space had opened the door to celebrations, community meals, and opportunities.

John checked his phone. "I gotta bounce. Work to do. If you get a call this week from Luna St. James, she's our wedding planner."

"Before you go, one more thing?"

"Yeah."

"Did Towanda send you and Chablis a gift to congratulate you on your engagement?"

John laughed. "Oh, yeah. Check this out. Like a week after we got engaged, Chablis came home after work and her neighbor brought her this big box, right? Chablis opened it and there was a congratulations note from Towanda and two matching white spa robes in a box from Saks Fifth Avenue."

"Classy."

"Yeah, classy, but that's not all." He shifted his gaze around the room, then leaned in closer. "I thought the robes were generous. Why did Chablis take them out and find a copy of *Love Worth Making: How To Have Ridiculously Great Sex in a Long-Lasting Relationship* underneath?"

Gabriel laughed. "*Love Worth Making*? Hope you both have a good time."

"We plan to. Most definitely."

In the thinkLARGE reception area, Jackie held up a finger and nodded to him while she finished a phone call.

He waited. Hands clasped behind his back. Grateful he had Antonio back at eatLARGE, holding him down so he could take care of business.

She hung up and pulled off her black reading glasses. "Hello, Chef Gabriel. To what do we owe this honor?"

"Good afternoon, Jackie. I'd here to meet with Towanda. Is she available?"

"She's on a conference call with Mrs. Brown and her daughters at the moment. How long are you able to wait?"

Gabriel shifted his weight from foot to foot. He'd rushed over, thinking Towanda would be available to talk with him right away. So stupid. She's a CEO. Just because she could have brunch with him on short notice, didn't mean all her time was that accessible. Mariah had already mentioned she'd packed her calendar with activity. And he had his own career to handle as well. He should have called. Calling made perfect sense, except that the urge to look at Towanda face-to-face drove him. He had to see her. But she was busy and he should leave. No. Wait. No. Leave a long message with Jackie. He couldn't do that. No.

Jackie looked just as confused as he felt. "Chef Gabriel?"

"Yes."

"Is something wrong?"

"Gabriel?"

He whipped around and Towanda stood in her office doorway. She wore a white double-breasted blazer dress and matching heels. Hair straightened and pulled into a tight bun. Understated silver jewelry. He envisioned her on a *Black Enterprise* cover. Curvaceous and courageous. Powerful and tough, but generous and sweet. A human baklava, with layer after layer of filling and syrup and honey.

White AirPods in her ears, she nodded to Jackie and waved Gabriel toward into office in one smooth move.

He sat in the leather chair in front of her desk. Waiting again. This time he rested his hands on his knees to keep from jogging his legs up and down.

Towanda spoke to the air. "Ladies, please keep the discussion going.

I need to mute briefly, but I'll return in a few minutes." She pressed her left ear pod. Looked at him. Eyes wide. "Gabriel, is there an emergency with eatLARGE?"

"No."

"Good," She exhaled and dropped into her chair. "I'm on a client call, but when I heard your voice and opened the door and you were standing there, I almost had a heart attack. How come you didn't call first?"

"I needed to talk to you in person."

"Why?"

Risk. Towanda understood risk. Had scrambled and cooked risk for breakfast the moment she entered the restaurant space and put him in charge.

He hadn't risked a thing.

Time to change that.

Gabriel leaned forward and gazed past her rimless glasses, into her brown eyes. "I live with my Aunt Abigail because she and Uncle Smitty were the only ones willing to let me stay with them after I left prison. Big house in West Philly. Across from the School of the Future. I stay on the third floor, but that's about to change on July first. I buy my clothes at Macy's and my shoes at DSW. I don't care about fashion. I don't own diamonds, but I'm not in debt." He paused. "After I got sentenced, my mom told me I could rot in prison. My dad didn't accept calls from me. My girl moved on and had somebody else's baby. My friends either died or scattered. I don't know where they are and don't care to find out. I've had to walk away from women who were only interested in me staying in that hustling life. The kitchen and the Christians were all that got me through." He paused again, took a cleansing breath, and kept going. "No one ever bought me anything like that Movado watch, not without expecting something in return. Everything I have, I worked my butt off to pay for. I've never encountered that kind of love and generosity. I didn't understand it and I'm sorry."

Towanda sat open-mouthed and blinking.

Gabriel stood up, arms at his sides. "I've been protecting myself, but that's stupid. You already know how I feel about you, and I've missed you and the moments that felt so right when I spent time with you. We were like water for chocolate."

"Like what?"

"*Like Water for Chocolate*. It's a novel about passion and recipes. I read it years ago." He pointed to her phone. "I think your muted minutes should end. You owe Mrs. Brown your attention. Whenever I had your attention, I treasured it, and if I have the chance to have that again, I choose you." He moved toward the door. Turned back. "Tell Mrs. Brown Chef Gabriel says you look stunning wearing her new makeup line."

CHAPTER 19

Towanda

Towanda kicked her heels off and pushed them to the side. She slid her laptop bag down next to them. Home sweet home.

AirPods in, she spoke to Mariah through bluetooth. "I learned more about that man in a one minute conversation than I have in a full year."

Mariah asked, "And you didn't say anything back?"

"I couldn't figure out what to say."

"He lost his friends and his family. Who would have thought?"

"I didn't think, bestie. I didn't." Towanda released her hair from the bun and let her strands fall down loose. Barefoot and free and striding into the kitchen. "I spent all that time building the restaurant with him and I never pried about his family background. He's always been so even and steady around me. So professional minded."

"Remind you of anyone you know?"

"I guess we're two peas in a pod, because you know I don't walk around telling random people about my dad's overdose or my mama abandoning me." Towanda rested her hand on the refrigerator door, but didn't open it. "Family hurt. And he held me with so much tenderness that day."

"He who? What happened?"

"The afternoon David called eatLARGE to find me. After I talked with him, I broke down in Gabriel's arms and he held and rocked me."

"Now I remember, but I wasn't focused on Gabriel then—"

"Because of David and Shayna—"

"Yeah, Gabriel was there for me the whole time, but I was so excited to hear something about my mama and I was standing there talking to a brother I didn't even know I had...I don't think I stopped to ask Gabriel why he'd been okay holding me for so long."

"From what you're telling me, he's had times in his life when he needed someone to hold him and rock him."

"All of that." Towanda opened the fridge and scanned the shelves. The cleaner had made everything immaculate. Items from her grocery delivery were stacked neatly inside.

No onions.

She shut the refrigerator door and looked across the counter to the wire baskets. Two of them. One with white onions. One with yellow onions. She'd left a note for Yolanda to make sure the items always remained at room temperature.

"Mariah?"

"Umm-hmm."

"He said he'd choose me again if he had the chance."

"Okay?"

She paused. "What do you think? Should I give him one?"

"Up to you. I think you'll have a really difficult time finding anyone else with the wit, manners, skills, tenderness and let's not forget the height to walk alongside you daily and deal with your outstanding traits and your bad ones."

"My onions are on the counter."

"Now I think you've flown right past wondering and landed on planet crazy. Call that man. I'm hanging up."

With Mariah off the line, Towanda walked away, leaving her phone on the kitchen island.

She showered and washed and conditioned her hair to make the curls come back to life. Changed into a pink silk lounging outfit. Used the Caviar app to have spicy tuna sushi delivered. Ate the sushi. Sorted through mail. Opened the important envelopes. Sent the junk mail through the shredder.

Nighttime grew darker and comfortable enough for Towanda to pick up the phone again.

She laid on the sofa, flat on her back, staring up. What she saw instead of a snow-colored ceiling were all the moments she'd experienced with Gabriel. When he ducked his head, walking through the front door of the soon-to-be eatLARGE space. Her first time tasting his delectable food. His arms around her after speaking to David. Their business interactions. Food tasting at eatLARGE. Church and lunch and those wonderful kisses. Him holding her and her holding him back and taking everything slowly but surely.

She dialed and reached his voicemail. Ended the call.

Something was missing.

Her knees met the floor and supported her body when she kneeled, face to the sofa cushions.

Head down and hands clasped, she prayed. "I'm not a perfect woman, Lord. I never will be. Lead me and guide me, Lord, I surrender. I surrender my heart and motivations, and my desires, worries, and fears. My life has always been in your hands. Love has to be in your hands, and I don't care how lonely I feel sometimes, I'm not choosing anyone without your leadership. I'm dropping my pride and my heart is open wide. My prayer to you is simple, Lord. Lead me. Lead me into the future that you want for me. It could include Gabriel, or not include him, but either way, I thank you for the confusion, because it's causing me to seek you. Where you lead, I will follow. Thank you, Lord. I love you. Amen."

CHAPTER 20

Gabriel

A mocha-colored young woman with waist-length braids and a fluttery red dress said, "All the guests are seated outdoors and dinner will start momentarily." Her nails clicked against laptop keys. "May I have your name, sir?"

He adjusted his tie. Red for the occasion. "Gabriel Seay."

"Seay." Her eyes caught something on the screen that must have triggered her sudden smile. "I'm so pleased to meet you, Chef Gabriel. My name is Niambi Bryant. Welcome to our Red, White, and Blue Family Extravaganza."

"Thank you. I'm thankful to be here."

He stepped back and stood to the side of the room while Niambi used a walkie-talkie to summon someone named Edison to escort him to the garden.

Gabriel hadn't expected so many checkpoints for a family reunion, but he probably should have. From what Towanda had mentioned in April, the Red, White, and Blue Extravaganza would look more like a mini *Essence* festival than a humble family-friendly event. So far, she hadn't lied. He'd spied the huge white outdoor tents from the taxi window. Inside the gray stone cottage, roses in crystal vases filled the room. Their flowery fragrance permeated the air.

A stocky brown-skinned teen with a Colgate smile walked over and extended his hand. "Chef Gabriel Seay from Philadelphia. I'm Edison Bryant. I'm from Raleigh, North Carolina. The Bryant family are first cousins to the Mathis family. We're so grateful to have you with us this weekend."

Gabriel shook his hand. Firm grip. "Grateful to be here."

"Will you follow me, please?"

Gabriel trailed Edison. A hospitality cottage? Imported roses? Teenaged hosts with impeccable training and manners? Gabriel braced himself. He wouldn't be surprised if a red carpet and paparazzi awaited him. As if the tents, greeting house, and roses didn't impress him enough.

They reached the end of the hallway, and Gabriel exhaled. French doors were covered with white roses and ivy. No paparazzi. Only a set of wide stone stairs that lead to a lawn so thick and green it resembled a carpet. An older, bald, brown-skinned brother waited at the bottom of the staircase. His red tie matched Edison's.

Gabriel asked, "Let me guess. I'm about to meet your dad?"

Edison gave a slight bow. "Yes, that's my father, Dr. Edison Bryant. He'll take care of you from here. Please enjoy your time with our family."

Checkpoint number three reached out with another firm handshake. "My daughter tells me I am meeting Chef Gabriel Seay from Philadelphia."

"Yes sir. Good to meet you."

"The pleasure is all mine, and welcome," Dr. Bryant said. "Two tents over and you will find your date. You're seated right next to her. You've missed cocktail hour, but you can let your dinner server know what you'd like to drink."

"I expected printed colorful t-shirts. Barbecue pits. The *Electric Slide*. Your family has done an incredible job here."

"I like to think I belong to a family that works hard. When we collaborate, we like to give each other the very best." Dr. Bryant leaned over. Lowered his voice. "Between you and me, some of the family are stuffier than others. Hang out late tonight and a bunch of us will have that barbecue and a good Spades game going on."

Gabriel laughed. "I hear you, doc. Loud and clear."

"Enjoy yourself."

Gabriel turned away and looked past the first tent to the second tent, and he spied her. Beautiful. Radiant. A wide-brimmed red hat graced her head. Classy as always, and sitting at table covered in spotless white linen and decorated with red and white roses and greenery. A cutie-pie little girl perched on her lap, whispering in her ear.

She broke out in a grin when he reached her side. "My darling, I'd been wondering when you would make it."

He bent down and kissed her soft cheek. "I miscalculated my travel time from the ferry. Forgive me, Nana."

"You're forgiven," she beamed. "Sit, sit. You came all this way. Take a load off and get ready for a wonderful dinner that you didn't have to make."

Munchkin kept her skinny arms wrapped tight around Nana's neck. She scrunched her tiny nose at him.

Gabriel sat and stretched his legs beneath the table. He nodded toward the girl. "Your great granddaughter?"

"How did you guess?"

"She won't let you go."

"Yes, this is Lilianne's youngest daughter, Jasmine. She has two boys and two girls. And I think a fifth might be on the way, but don't get me to lying."

Gabriel ducked his head. Tried to erase eagerness from his face. "Where's Towanda?"

"Way over there, seated under a different tent, close to the podium and microphone. She's involved with a presentation tonight. Lilianne gave her a portion of the family history speech. Most of the cousins have a small part."

"Sounds lovely."

Nana rolled her eyes. "Sounds long. If I fall asleep, don't pay me any mind. Just shake me if I snore."

He patted her wrinkled hand. "I'll cover you with a blanket."

"Now then, did you agree to the terms that work for you?"

Gabriel whistled. "Nana, it was the hardest decision I've ever made, but I had to do it. It's best for all of us, you know. Me. Towanda. The restaurant family. But, what if—"

She shushed him. "Eh, eh? No questions. You did the right thing."

"She's going to be okay?"

"She's my amazing granddaughter, and she's better than okay." Nana hugged Jasmine tight. Rocked her. "I raised her that way."

CHAPTER 21

Towanda

Towanda didn't need index cards to remember her family speech. She'd learned how to memorize talking points ten years earlier at Toastmasters. Still, she'd stood at the podium and glanced to the side twice, and there was Lilianne, teeth clenched and painted eyebrows raised, waiting for Towanda to mess up.

Her cousin should have sipped a mint iced tea and relaxed.

Towanda wouldn't let her family down.

She smiled and segued into her ending lines. "We are Mathises. We are Bryants. We are Womacks. We are Earley's. We are Thomases. We are every unknown name of an enslaved person before Joseph C. Mathis and his wife, Patience. All names, faces, skin tones, marriages, babies, and more. We wear red tonight to represent the blood of those who have come before us and those yet to come. Thank you for attending. May God bless our family."

The applause hit her ears. Towanda glanced sidelong. Lilianne clapped and cheered with a *praise the Lord hallelujah thank you Jesus* look on her face.

Towanda mouthed *thank you.*

Crowd sounds escalated from polite applause to whistles and cheers.

Lilianne stopped clapping. Blood drained from her pecan-brown face. Lip movements exaggerated, she mouthed *turn around now* to Towanda.

Slowly, Towanda faced the crowd again.

Gabriel stood tall on the grassy area by the makeshift stage. He wore a crimson-colored tie. His suit must have been tailored, because the fabric hit all the right areas of his body perfectly. He held red blooming roses.

She blinked. "Gabriel."

"Towanda."

"When did you get here?"

He shouted past the cheers. "What?"

"When?"

"What?"

"Hold on!"

Towanda kicked off her red shoes, gathered her silky hem in her fist and hopped down from the stage. Mind dazed. Giddy. Transfixed. She ran to the man who made her heart beat double time when she first laid eyes on him.

She reached him and stopped. Gazed up. Sighed. "Gabriel."

"Towanda."

"How?"

"Nana."

"I should have known." She grinned. "That lady will outlive us all. She's so crafty."

"She's exceptional, and you're just like her."

"You're not so bad yourself."

He smiled. "Towanda, I am your number one fan. I love you, and since I'm standing here in front of your family, I'm thinking we should have talked about our family plans."

"Plans?"

He stepped close enough for her to smell his Dior Sauvage. "One of my fantasies is to be a girl dad. Daughters. Three or four. One must be named Madeline. Do what you need in order to prepare. We have to take enough time to interview the best nanny."

Towanda laughed. Put her hand on her hip. "Um? Dating? Marriage? Where did that go? You moved right to bouncing baby girls."

He laid the flowers down on the grass. Pulled her so tight into his firm embrace that she could feel his heart thumping.

"Ms. Mathis, we aren't getting any younger." He landed a kiss on her forehead. "Like I said, do what you need to do to prepare, and that includes getting to know one another better. But you should know that Nana wants all the girls to learn to play UNO stacksies."

She stood on tiptoe and kissed his cheek. "My lawyer called this morning. The I's are dotted and the T's are crossed."

"I never wanted to believe my own hype, but I guess some of it's real. If it wasn't, those private investors wouldn't have partnered with me for the venture. They just sent the check to LARGE Enterprises. All done. I'm sure you'll use the money to invest in another great creative adventure."

"How do you think you'll enjoy being an owner?"

"Owner *and* chief investor, and I'll take it day by day. When I expand to more locations, I'll extend more work opportunities to the people who need them. Flex my mentoring muscles. I saw restaurant space close to the Philadelphia Zoo."

"You're thinking like an entrepreneur. Got your eye on opportunity. You know that area is gentrifying."

"Then Philly definitely needs one of my restaurants over there."

She squeezed him tight and whispered. "My family is still watching us. We should give them what they're waiting for."

He whispered, "I love you, and that means you will never cook another meal for the rest of your life."

"I love you, and I hadn't planned to," she whispered back.

CHAPTER 22

Towanda & Gabriel

"Wanda, come out of that bathroom or I'm coming in there," Gabriel said. "Do we need to go home early?"

"No, I'll be fine. And could you please not say *home* so loudly? Chablis and John might hear you, and this is their day. We agreed not to upstage them."

"Chablis and John are cutting wedding cake. I guarantee you neither one of them are thinking about us." Gabriel jiggled the door handle. "Baby, seriously."

Towanda gripped the sides of the pedestal sink. "It's only a nausea feeling, and it's passing. I'll be okay. This is new for me."

"Need a ginger ale?"

"Please."

"Be right back."

Towanda straightened up and viewed in the oval-shaped silver mirror. She was indeed glowing, like Gabriel had whispered that morning during their shower time. He'd massaged her hips and belly and assured her he didn't care if she developed stretch marks. He'd love her body no matter how much it changed.

The nausea feeling subsided. Thank God for Gabriel, because she still needed that ginger ale. And thank God for Chablis' friend Daisy and her beautiful borrowed mansion. The first floor powder room was practically a work of art. What a wonderful place to hold a wedding picnic. If Towanda had to feel sick and dash off anywhere, she was grateful to enter a comfortable, private room that smelled of lavender.

"Wanda?" Gabriel knocked. "Baby, I have your drink. Plenty of ice."

She opened the door and took the plastic cup. "Ugh. I thought it was called morning sickness because it was supposed to happen in the morning. The sun's about to go down."

Gabriel lay his hand against his wife's abdomen. "It's possible little Madeline doesn't know her days from her nights yet."

Towanda sipped ginger ale. Swallowed. "Keep your feelings in check, honey. We're months away from the ultrasound and I don't want you moping if Dr. Taube tells us to get ready for our son."

"Or twins."

"Please, no."

"So anyway, Maddie could double her size right about now."

"It happens that fast?"

"As fast as everything else, I'm sure."

Towanda gazed in her husband's eyes and melted. She touched his thick mustache. Ran her fingers over his strong jawline. Leaned close and let his body's warmth soothe her even more. Gave him a light kiss.

"That's all I get?" He took the cup back and placed it on the hall table. Pulled her body into the wingspan of his embrace and buried his nose in her hair. "We should say our goodbyes soon. I need to get you home and rub your feet for a while."

She laced her fingers into his. "Maybe we could have a reprise from this morning? It was heaven."

"Really? And I thought sundown in Aruba was the ultimate touch-down moment."

"Stop."

"Are you sure you don't want a wedding? Something small but elegant?"

"With a protruding belly?"

"We can pull something together before the end of the month. You're not showing yet."

Towanda kissed Gabriel's lips. Pulled her hands from his and placed them on his chest. "No thank you. Marrying in Aruba was the best decision we could have ever made. Neither one of us needs the aggravation of wedding planning. We're selling a condo. Getting a nursery ready at the new place. Expanding your restaurant. I don't think we need one more thing to do before we become parents."

"All right, Ms. Mathis-Seay. Can we at least wear our rings around the fam?"

"Tomorrow. Then let the questions about elopement begin. Chablis warned me that when Pastor Downes finds out, we'll have to complete marriage counseling."

"Well, if we do that, then I'm definitely pressing for a wedding. It doesn't have to be big. I'll ask Jackie how your calendar looks around Valentine's Day."

She grinned. "I'll be huge, but Valentine's Day sounds sweet. Can we do it in Franklin Square? I want David and Shayna to give me away to you, and we need a violinist to play "A Long Walk"."

"Of course."

Towanda held her husband's face and gave him kiss after probing kiss. Transferred her heart and soul into those light touches, then stepped back and stared in his eyes again.

"Gabriel."

"Towanda."

"The Seays are going home in fifteen minutes."

He took her hand and winked. "I thought you'd see it my way."

Gabriel led Towanda to the mansion's patio. October sunset. Daylight succumbed to a navy blue night sky. Towanda clutched Gabriel's hand and watched her friends dance and celebrate a newly united couple.

In a few days, word would be out that there were two newlyweds to celebrate. One with a new person to present to the world in seven months. She shivered at the notion.

Towanda Mathis-Seay.

Wife and mother.

My life is a beautiful tornado, Towanda thought. *I never know which way the winds will blow, but I'm still enjoying every minute.*

Leave a Review

Dear Reader,

I hope you enjoy this story. Book reviews are a wonderful way for readers to connect with authors, and they also play a crucial role in helping us spread the word about our stories.

Whether you loved the book or even liked it a little bit, a quick review on the platform where you purchased it would be incredibly helpful. Even if you received a complimentary copy your honest feedback is valuable.

Of course, I'd also love to hear your thoughts directly. Feel free to reach out at kl@klgilchrist.com!

Warmly,
K.L. Gilchrist

Acknowledgments

Hello, dear reader! Whether you bought this story through an online bookseller or borrowed it from a library, *thank you for reading.*

Lynn and LaKeisha — you made me do it. Thanks for adoring Towanda Mathis and asking for more details about her life. When she met six foot plus Gabriel Seay, you and others rooted for them to fall in love. The talented chef now holds his commanding curvy woman in his arms and the bossy chick has her man.

Chris — your support means everything to me. Once again, bless you for putting up with my early mornings and my late nights and for reading every draft. You become a single parent whenever I go deep undercover with a book. Bless you, for being my biggest fan and my true love.

To anyone who reads these words: thank you sincerely for supporting literary entertainment for people of faith. To God be the glory!

Subscribe To My Newsletter

How will you find out about my latest releases, read reviews for recommended books by other Christian fiction authors, and more? By becoming an author newsletter subscriber! You can sign up on my website at klgilchrist.com. As a gift, all newsletter subscribers immediately receive the free short story collection *Five For The Journey: Stories*

This eBook is not published publicly. It is only available to subscribers. So sign up today!

About the Author

K.L. Gilchrist crafts true-to-life contemporary tales for women of faith. The author of *Broken Together* and other stories enjoys bringing order to chaos and dancing whenever and wherever she can. She and her family call the suburbs of Philadelphia, PA home. Feel free to visit her online at www.klgilchrist.com.

facebook.com/402435140151793
x.com/KL_Gilchrist
instagram.com/klgilchrist

www.ingramcontent.com/pod-product-compliance
Lightning Source LLC
Chambersburg PA
CBHW030816200726
48288CB00004B/1259